D0962152

YOU ARE NOT A STRANGER HERE

NAN A. TALESE

DOUBLEDAY

NEW YORK LONDON TORONTO SYDNEY AUCKLAND

YOU ARE NOT A STRANGER HERE

ADAM HASLETT

PUBLISHED BY NAN A. TALESE

an imprint of Doubleday
a division of Random House, Inc.
1540 Broadway, New York, New York 10036

DOUBLEDAY is a trademark of Doubleday
a division of Random House, Inc.

Some of the stories in this book have appeared, in different form, in the following publications: "Notes to My Biographer" in *Zoetrope All-Story,* "Devotion" in *The Yale Review,* "War's End" in *BOMB* magazine, "The Beginnings of Grief" in *The James White Review,* and "Reunion" in *The Alembic.*

The quote that appears on pages 184–185 is from the novel *Affliction* by Russell Banks.

Book design by Gretchen Achilles

Library of Congress Cataloging-in-Publication Data

Haslett, Adam. You are not a stranger here / Adam Haslett.
p. cm.
I. Title.

PS3608.A85 Y68 2002
813'.6—dc21
2001054839

ISBN 0-385-50167-6

PRINTED IN THE UNITED STATES OF AMERICA

August 2002
FIRST EDITION

1 3 5 7 9 10 8 6 4 2

TO MY FAMILY

AND

TO JENNIFER CHANDLER-WARD,

LOVE ALWAYS

CONTENTS

YOU ARE

NOT A STRANGER

HERE

NOTES TO MY BIOGRAPHER

TWO THINGS TO get straight from the beginning: I hate doctors and have never joined a support group in my life. At seventy-three, I'm not about to change. The mental health establishment can go screw itself on a barren hilltop in the rain before I touch their snake oil or listen to the visionless chatter of men half my age. I have shot Germans in the fields of Normandy, filed twenty-six patents, married three women, survived them all, and am currently the subject of an investigation by the IRS, which has about as much chance of collecting from me as Shylock did of getting his pound of flesh. Bureaucracies have trouble thinking clearly. I, on the other hand, am perfectly lucid.

Note, for instance, how I obtained the SAAB I'm presently driving into the Los Angeles basin: a niece in Scottsdale lent it to me. Do you think she'll ever see it again? Unlikely. Of course when I borrowed it from her I had every intention of returning it and in a few days or weeks I may feel that way again, but for now forget her and her husband and three children who looked at me over the kitchen table like I was a museum piece sent to bore them. I could run circles around those kids. They're spoon-fed Ritalin and private schools and have eyes that say give me things I don't have. I wanted to read them a book on the history of the world, its migrations, plagues, and wars, but the shelves of their outsized condominium were full of ceramics and biographies of the stars. The whole thing depressed the hell out of me and I'm glad to be gone.

A week ago I left Baltimore with the idea of seeing my son, Graham. I've been thinking about him a lot recently, days we spent together in the barn at the old house, how with him as my audience ideas came quickly; I don't know when I'll get to see him again. I thought I might as well catch up with some of the other relatives along the way and planned to start at my daughter, Linda's, in Atlanta but when I arrived it turned out she'd moved. I called Graham and when he got over the shock of hearing my voice, he said Linda didn't want to see me. By the time my younger brother, Ernie, refused to do anything more than have lunch with me after I'd taken a bus all the way to Houston, I began to get the idea this episodic reunion thing might be more trouble than it was worth. Scottsdale did nothing to alter my opinion. These people seem to think they'll have another chance, that I'll be coming around again. The fact is I've completed my will, made bequests of my patent rights, and am now just composing a few notes to my biographer, who, in a few decades, when the true influence of my work becomes apparent, may need them to clarify certain issues.

- Franklin Caldwell Singer, b. 1924, Baltimore, Maryland.
- Child of a German machinist and a banker's daughter.
- My psych discharge following "desertion" in Paris was trumped up by an army intern resentful of my superior knowledge of the diagnostic manual. The nude dancing incident at the Louvre in a room full of Rubenses had occurred weeks earlier and was of a piece with other celebrations at the time.
- B.A., Ph.D., engineering, Johns Hopkins University.
- 1952. First and last electroshock treatment for which I will never, never, never forgive my parents.
- 1954–1965. Researcher, Eastman Kodak Laborato-

ries. As with so many institutions in this country, talent was resented. I was fired as soon as I began to point out flaws in the management structure. Two years later I filed a patent on a shutter mechanism that Kodak eventually broke down and purchased (then–vice president for product development Arch Vendellini *WAS* having an affair with his daughter's best friend, contrary to what he will tell you. Notice the way his left shoulder twitches when he's lying).

- All subsequent diagnoses—and let me tell you, there have been a number—are the result of two forces, both in their way pernicious: (1) the attempt by the psychiatric establishment over the last century to redefine eccentricity as illness, and (2) the desire of members of my various families to render me docile and if possible immobile.

- The electric bread slicer concept was stolen from me by a man in a diner in Chevy Chase dressed as a reindeer who I could not possibly have known was an employee of Westinghouse.

- That I have no memories of the years 1988–1990 and believed until very recently that Ed Meese was still the attorney general is not owing to my purported paranoid blackout but on the contrary to the fact my third wife took it upon herself to lace my coffee with tranquilizers. Believe nothing you hear about the divorce settlement.

When I ring the buzzer at Graham's place in Venice, a Jew in his late twenties with some fancy-looking musculature answers the door. He appears nervous and says, "We weren't expecting you till tomorrow," and I ask him who *we* are and he says, "Me and Graham," adding hurriedly, "We're friends, you know, only friends. I don't live here, I'm just over to use the computer."

All I can think is I hope this guy isn't out here trying to get acting jobs, because it's obvious to me right away that my son is gay and is screwing this character with the expensive-looking glasses. There was a lot of that in the military and I learned early on that it comes in all shapes and sizes, not just the fairy types everyone expects. Nonetheless, I am briefly shocked by the idea that my twenty-nine-year-old boy has never seen fit to share with me the fact that he is a fruitcake—no malice intended—and I resolve right away to talk to him about it when I see him. Marlon Brando overcomes his stupor and lifting my suitcase from the car leads me through the back garden past a lemon tree in bloom to a one-room cottage with a sink and plenty of light to which I take an instant liking.

"This will do nicely," I say and then I ask him, "How long have you been sleeping with my son?" It's obvious he thinks I'm some brand of geriatric homophobe getting ready to come on in a religiously heavy manner and seeing that deer-caught-in-the-headlights look in his eye I take pity and disabuse him. I've seen women run down by tanks. I'm not about to get worked up about the prospect of fewer grandchildren. When I start explaining to him that social prejudice of all stripes runs counter to my Enlightenment ideals—ideals tainted by centuries of partial application—it becomes clear to me that Graham has given him the family line. His face grows patient and his smile begins to leak the sympathy of the ignorant: poor old guy suffering from mental troubles his whole life, up one month, down the next, spewing grandiose notions that slip like sand through his fingers, to which I always say, you just look up Frank Singer at the U.S. Patent Office. In any case, this turkey probably thinks the Enlightenment is a marketing scheme for General Electric; I spare him the seminar I could easily conduct and say, "Look, if the two of you share a bed, it's fine with me."

"That drive must have worn you out," he says hopefully. "Do you want to lie down for a bit?"

I tell him I could hook a chain to my niece's SAAB and drag it through a marathon. This leaves him nonplussed. We walk back across the yard together into the kitchen of the bungalow. I ask him for pen, paper, and a calculator and begin sketching an idea that came to me just a moment ago—I can feel the presence of Graham already—for a bicycle capable of storing the energy generated on the downward slope in a small battery and releasing it through a handlebar control when needed on the uphill—a potential gold mine when you consider the aging population and the increase in leisure time created by early retirement. I have four pages of specs and the estimated cost of a prototype done by the time Graham arrives two hours later. He walks into the kitchen wearing a blue linen suit, a briefcase held to his chest, and seeing me at the table goes stiff as a board. I haven't seen him in five years and the first thing I notice is that he's got bags under his eyes.

When I open my arms to embrace him he takes a step backward.

"What's the matter?" I ask. Here is my child wary of me in a strange kitchen in California, his mother's ashes spread long ago over the Potomac, the objects of our lives together stored in boxes or sold.

"You actually came," he says.

"I've invented a new bicycle," I say but this seems to reach him like news of some fresh death. Eric hugs Graham there in front of me. I watch my son rest his head against this fellow's shoulder like a tired soldier on a train. "It's going to have a self-charging battery," I say, sitting again at the table to review my sketches.

WITH GRAHAM HERE my idea is picking up speed and while he's in the shower I unpack my bags, rearrange the furniture in the cottage, and tack my specs to the wall. Returning to the house, I ask Eric if I can use the phone and he says that's fine and then he tells me, "Graham hasn't been sleeping so great lately, but I know he really does want to see you."

"Sure, no hard feelings, fine."

"He's been dealing with a lot recently. Maybe some things you could talk to him about . . . and I think you might—"

"Sure, sure, no hard feelings," and then I call my lawyer, my engineer, my model builder, three advertising firms whose numbers I find in the yellow pages, the American Association of Retired Persons—that market will be key—an old college friend who I remember once told me he'd competed in the

Tour de France, figuring he'll know the bicycle industry angle, my bank manager to discuss financing, the patent office, the Cal Tech physics lab, the woman I took to dinner the week before I left Baltimore, and three local liquor stores before I find one that will deliver a case of Dom Pérignon.

"That'll be for me!" I call out to Graham as he emerges from the bedroom to answer the door what seems only minutes later. He moves slowly and seems sapped of life.

"What's this?"

"We're celebrating! There's a new project in the pipeline!"

Graham stares at the bill as though he's having trouble reading it. Finally, he says, "This is twelve hundred dollars. We're not buying it."

I tell him Schwinn will drop that on doughnuts for the sales reps when I'm done with this bike, that Oprah Winfrey's going to ride it through the halftime show at the Super Bowl.

"There's been a mistake," he says to the delivery guy.

I end up having to go outside and pay for it through the window of the truck with a credit card the man is naive enough to accept and I carry it back to the house myself.

"What am I going to do?" I hear Graham whisper.

I round the corner into the kitchen and they fall silent. The two of them make a handsome couple standing there in the gauzy, expiring light of evening. When I was born you could have arrested them for kissing. There ensues an argument that I only half bother to participate in concerning the champagne and my enthusiasm, a recording he learned from his mother; he presses play and the fraction of his ancestry that suffered from conventionalism speaks through his mouth like a ventriloquist: Your-idea-is-fantasy-calm-down-it-will-be-the-ruin-of-you-medication-medication-medication. He has a good mind, my son, always has, and somewhere the temerity to use it, to spear mediocrity in the eye, but in a world that encourages nothing of the sort, the curious boy becomes the anxious man. He must suffer his people's regard for appearances. Sad. I begin to articulate this with diamond-like precision, which seems only to exacerbate the situation.

"Why don't we have some champagne?" Eric interjects. "You two can talk this over at dinner."

An admirable suggestion. I take three glasses from the cupboard, remove a bottle from the case, pop the cork, fill the glasses, and propose a toast to their health.

My niece's SAAB does eighty-five without a shudder on the way to dinner. With the roof down, smog blowing through my hair, I barely hear Graham who's shouting something from the passenger's seat. He's probably worried about a ticket, which for the high of this ride I'd pay twice over and tip the officer to boot. Sailing down the freeway I envision a lane of bicycles quietly recycling efficiencies once lost to the simple act of pedaling. We'll have to get the environmentalists involved which could mean government money for research and a lobbying arm to navigate any legislative interference. Test marketing in L.A. will increase the chance of celebrity endorsements and I'll probably need to do a book on the germination of the idea for release with the first wave of product. I'm thinking early next year. The advertising tag line hits me as we glide beneath an overpass: *Make Every Revolution Count.*

There's a line at the restaurant and when I try to slip the maître d' a twenty, Graham holds me back.

"Dad," he says, "you can't do that."

"Remember the time I took you to the Ritz and you told me the chicken in your sandwich was tough and I spoke to the manager and we got the meal for free? And you drew a diagram of the tree fort you wanted and it gave me an idea for storage containers."

He nods his head.

"Come on, where's your smile?"

I walk up to the maître d' but when I hand him the twenty he gives me a funny look and I tell him he's a lousy shit for pretending he's above that sort of thing. "You want a hundred?" I ask and am about to give him an even larger piece of my mind when Graham turns me around and says, "Please don't."

"What kind of work are you doing?" I ask him.

"Dad," he says, "just settle down." His voice is so quiet, so meek.

"I asked you what kind of work you do."

"I work at a brokerage."

A brokerage! What didn't I teach this kid? "What do you do for them?"

"Stocks. Listen, Dad, we need—"

"Stocks!" I say. "Christ! Your mother would turn in her grave if she had one."

"Thanks," he says under his breath.

"What was that?" I ask.

"Forget it."

At this point, I notice everyone in the foyer is staring at us. They all look like they were in television twenty years ago, the men wearing Robert Wagner turtlenecks and blazers. A woman in mauve hot pants with a shoulder bag the size of her torso appears particularly disapproving and self-satisfied and I feel like asking her what it is she does to better the lot of humanity. "You'll be riding my bicycle in three years," I tell her. She draws back as though I had thrown a rat on the carpet.

Once we're seated it takes ten minutes to get bread and water on the table and sensing a bout of poor service I begin to jot on a napkin the time of each of our requests and the hour of its arrival. Also, as it occurs to me:

- Hollow-core chrome frame with battery mounted over rear tire, wired to rear wheel engine housing, wired to handlebar control/thumb-activated accelerator. Warning to cyclist concerning increased speed of crankshaft during application of stored revolutions. Power brake?
- Biographer file: Graham as my muse, mystery thereof; see storage container, pancake press, tricycle engine, flying teddy bear, renovations of barn for him to play in, power bike.

Graham disagrees with me when I try to send back a second bottle of wine, apparently under the impression that one ought to accept spoiled goods in order not to hurt anybody's feelings. This strikes me as maudlin but I let it go for the sake of harmony. Something has changed in him. Appetizers take a startling nineteen minutes to appear.

"You should start thinking about quitting your job," I say. "I've decided I'm not going to stay on the sidelines with this one. The power bike's a flagship product, the kind of thing that could support a whole company. We stand to make a fortune, Graham, and I can do it with you." One of the Robert Wagners cranes his neck to look at me from a neighboring booth.

"Yeah, I bet you want a piece of the action, buddy," I say, which sends him back to his endive salad in a hurry. Graham listens as I elaborate the business plan: there's start-up financing, for which we'll easily attract venture capital, the choice of location for the manufacturing plant—you have to be careful about state regulations—executives to hire, designers to work under me, a sales team, accountants, benefits, desks, telephones, workshops, paychecks, taxes, computers, copiers, decor, watercoolers, doormats, parking spaces, electric bills. Maybe a humidifier. A lot to consider. As I speak, I notice that others in the restaurant are turning to listen as well. It's usually out of the corner of my eye that I see it, and the people disguise it well, returning to their conversations in what they probably think is convincing pantomime. The Westinghouse reindeer pops to mind. How ingenious they were to plant him there in the diner I ate at each Friday morning, knowing my affection for the Christmas myth, determined to steal my intellectual property.

- Re: Chevy Chase incident. Look also into whether or not I might have invented autoreverse tape decks and also therefore did Sony or GE own property adjacent to my Baltimore residence—noise, distraction tactics, phony road construction, etc., and also Schwinn, Raleigh, etc., presence during Los Angeles visit.

"Could we talk about something else?" Graham asks.

"Whatever you like," I say and then inform the waiter our entrées were twenty-six minutes in transit. Turns out my fish is tough as leather. The waiter's barely left when I have to begin snapping my fingers for his return.

"Stop that!" Graham says. I've reached the end of my tether with his passivity and freely ignore him. He's leaning over the table about to swat my arm down when the fellow returns.

"Is there a problem?"

"My halibut's dry as sand."

The goateed young man eyes my dish suspiciously as though I might have replaced the original plate with some duplicate entrée pulled from a bag beneath the table.

"I'll need a new one."

"No he won't," Graham says at once.

The waiter pauses, considering on whose authority to proceed.

"Do you have anything to do with bicycles?" I ask him.

"What do you mean?" he asks.

"Professionally."

The young man looks across the room to the maître d', who offers a coded nod.

"That's it. We're getting out of here," I say, grabbing bread rolls.

"Sit down," Graham insists.

But it's too late. I know the restaurant's lousy with mountain bike executives. "You think I'm going to let a bunch of industry hustlers steal an idea that's going to change the way every American and one day every person on the globe conceives of a bicycle? Do you realize what bicycles mean to people? They're like ice cream or children's stories, they're primal objects woven into the fabric of our earliest memories, not to mention our most intimate connection with the wheel itself an invention that marks the commencement of the great ascent of human knowledge that brought us through printing presses, religious transformations, undreamt-of speed, the moon. When you ride a bicycle you participate in an unbroken chain of human endeavor stretching back to stone-carting Egyptian peasants and I'm on the verge of revolutionizing that invention, making its almost mythical power a storable quantity. You have the chance to be there with me—like stout Cortez when with eagle eyes/He stared at the Pacific—and all his men/Looked at each other with a wild surmise—/Silent, upon a peak in Darien. The things we'll see!"

Because I'm standing as I say this a quorum of the restaurant feels I'm addressing them as well and though I've slipped in giving them a research lead I can see in their awed expressions they know as I do not everyone can scale the high white peaks of real invention. Some—such as these—must sojourn in the lowlands where the air is thick with half measures and dreams die of inertia. Yes! It is true.

This seems to convince Graham we indeed need to leave. He throws some cash on the table and steers me by the arm out of the restaurant. We walk slowly along the boulevard. There's something sluggish about Graham, his rounded shoulders and bowed head.

"Look, there's a Japanese place right over there we can get maki rolls and teriyaki, maybe some blowfish, I can hear all about the brokerage, we might even think about whether your company wants to do the IPO on the bike venture, there could be an advantage—"

He shakes his head and keeps walking up the street, one of whose features is a truly remarkable plentitude of shapely women, and I am reminded of the pleasures of being single, glances and smiles being enjoyed without guilt and for that matter why not consummation? Maybe it's unseemly for a seventy-three-year-old to talk about erections but oh, do I get 'em! I'm thinking along these lines when we pass the lobby of a luxury hotel convention center kind of place and of course I'm also thinking trade shows and how far ahead you have to book those things, so I turn in and after a small protest Graham follows; I tell him I need to use the bathroom.

"I'd like to talk to the special events manager," I say to the girl behind the desk.

"I'm afraid he's only here during the day, sir," she replies with a blistering customer service smile, as though she were telling me exactly what I wanted to hear.

"Well, isn't that just wonderful," I say and she seems to agree that yes it is wonderful, wonderful that the special events manager of the Continental Royale keeps such regular hours, as though it were the confirmation of some beneficent natural order.

"I guess I'll just have to take a suite anyway and see him in the morning. My son and I will have a little room service dinner in privacy, where the sharks don't circle!"

Mild concern clouds the girl's face as she taps at her keyboard.

"The Hoover Suite is available on nineteen. That's six hundred and eighty dollars a night. Will that be all right?"

"Perfect."

When I've secured the keys I cross to where Graham's sitting on the couch.

"Dinner is served," I say with a bow.

"What are you talking about?"

"I got us a suite," I say, rattling the keys.

Graham rolls his eyes and clenches his fists.

"Dad!" There's something desperate in his voice.

"What!"

"Stop! Just stop! You're out of control. Why do you think Linda and Ernie don't want to see you, Dad, why do you think that is? Is it so surprising to you? They can't handle this! Mom couldn't handle this! Can't you see that? It's *selfish* of you not to see a doctor!" he shouts, pounding his fists on his thighs. "It's *selfish* of you not to take the drugs! *Selfish!*"

The lobby's glare has drained his face of color and about his unblinking eyes I can see the outlines of what will one day be the marks of age and then all of a sudden the corpse of my son lies prostrate in front of me, the years since we last saw each other tunneling out before me like some infinite distance, and I hear the whisper of a killing loneliness travel along its passage as though the sum total of every minute of his pain in every spare hour of every year was drawn in a single breath and held in this expiring moment. Tears well in my eyes. I am overcome.

Graham stands up from the couch, shaken by the force of his own words.

I rattle the keys. "We're going to enjoy ourselves."

"You have to give those back to the desk."

By the shoulders I grab him, my greatest invention. "We can do so much better," I say. I take him by the wrist and lead him to the elevator hearing his mother's voice behind us reminding me to keep him out of the rain. "I will," I mutter, "I will."

Robert Wagner is on the elevator with Natalie Wood but they've aged badly and one doesn't take to them anymore. She chews gum and appears uncomfortable in tight clothing. His turtlenecks have become worn. But I figure they know things, they've been here a long time. So I say to him, "Excuse me, you wouldn't know where I might call for a girl or two, would you? Actually what we need is a girl and a young man, my son here's gay."

"Dad!" Graham shouts. "I'm sorry," he says to the couple, now backed against the wall as though I were a gangster in one of their lousy B movies. "He's just had a lot to drink."

"The hell I have. You got a problem with my son being gay?" The elevator door opens and they scurry onto the carpet like bugs.

For a man who watched thousands starve and did jackshit about it, the Hoover Suite is aptly named. There are baskets of fruit, a stocked refrigerator, a full bar, faux rococo paintings over the beds, overstuffed chairs, and rugs that demand bare feet for the sheer pleasure of the touch.

"We can't stay here," Graham says as I flip my shoes across the room.

His voice is disconsolate. He seems to have lost his animation of a moment ago, something I don't think I can afford to do right now: the eviction notices in Baltimore, the collection agencies, the smell of the apartment. "We're just getting started," I say quickly.

Graham's sitting in an armchair across the room and as he bows his head I imagine he's praying that when he raises it again, things will be different. As a child he used to bring me presents in my study on the days I was leaving for a trip and he'd ask me not to go. They were books he'd found on the shelf and wrapped in Christmas paper.

I pick up the phone on the bedside table and get the front desk. "This is the Hoover Suite calling. I want the number of an agency that will provide us with a young man, someone intelligent and attractive—"

Graham rips the phone from my hand.

"What is it?" I say. His mother was always encouraging me to ask him questions. "What's it like to be gay, Graham? Why have you never told me?"

He stares at me dumbfounded.

"What? What?" I say.

"How can you ask me that after all this time?"

"I want to understand. Are you in love with this Eric fellow?"

"I thought you were dead! Do you even begin to realize? I thought my own father was dead. You didn't call for four years but I couldn't bear to find out, I couldn't bear to go and find you dead, and so it was like I was a child again and I just hoped there was an excuse. Four years, Dad, and now you just appear and you want to know what it's like to be gay?"

I run to the refrigerator, where among other things there is a decent Chardonnay, and with the help of a corkscrew I find by the sink I pour us two glasses. Graham doesn't seem to want his but I set it down beside him anyway.

"Oh, Graham. The phone company in Baltimore's awful."

He starts to cry. He looks so young as he weeps, as he did in the driveway of the old house on the afternoon I taught him to ride a bicycle, the dust from the drive settling on his wetted cheek and damp eyelashes later to be rinsed in the warm water of the bath as dusk settled over the field and we listened together to the sound of his mother in the kitchen running water, the murmur of the radio and the stillness of evening in the country, how he seemed to understand it as well as I.

"You know, Graham, they're constantly overcharging me and then once they take a line out it's like getting the Red Sea to part to have it reinstalled but in a couple of weeks when the bicycle patent comes through that'll be behind us, you and Linda and Ernie and I, we'll all go to London and stay at the Connaught and I'll show you Regent's Park where your mother and I rowed a boat on our honeymoon circling the little island there where the ducks all congregate and which was actually a little dirty come to think of it though you don't really think of ducks as dirty, they look so graceful on the water but in fact—" All of a sudden I don't believe it myself and I can hear my own voice in the room, hear its dry pitch, and I've lost my train of thought and I can't stop picturing the yard where Graham used to play with his friends by the purple lilac and the apple tree whose knotted branches held the planks of the fort which I was so happy for him to enjoy never having had one myself. He knew me then even in my bravest moments when his mother and siblings were afraid of what they didn't understand; he would sit on the stool in the crumbling barn watching me cover the chalkboard propped on the fender of the broken Studebaker, diagramming a world of possible objects, the solar vehicles and collapsible homes, our era distilled into its necessary devices, and in the evenings, sprawled on the floor of his room, he'd trace with delicate hands what he remembered of my design.

I see those same hands now spread on his thighs, nails bitten down, cuticles torn.

I don't know how to say good-bye.

In the village of Saint-Sever an old woman nursed my dying friend through the night. At dawn I kissed his cold forehead and kept marching.

In the yard of the old house the apple tree still rustles in the evening breeze.

"Graham."

"You want to know what it's like?" he says. "I'll tell you. It's worrying all the time that one day he's going to leave me. And you want to know why that is? It's got nothing to do with being gay. It's because I know Mom left *you*. I tell you it's selfish not to take the pills because I know. Because I take them. You understand, Dad? It's in me too. I don't want Eric to find me in a parking lot in the middle of the night in my pajamas talking to a stranger like Mom did. I don't want him to find me hanged. I used to cast fire from the tips of my fingers some weeks and burn everything in my path and it was all progress and it was all incredibly, incredibly beautiful. And some weeks I couldn't brush my hair. But I take the pills now, and I haven't bankrupted us yet, and I don't want to kill myself just now. I take them and I think of Eric. That's what it's like."

"But the fire, Graham? What about the fire?"

In his eyes, there is sadness enough to kill us both.

"Do you remember how you used to watch me do my sketches in the barn?"

Tears run down his cheeks as he nods.

"Let me show you something," I say. Across the room in the drawer of the desk I find a marker. It makes sense to me now, he can see what I see, he's always been able to. Maybe it doesn't have to end. I unhook a painting from the wall and set it on the floor. On the yellow wallpaper I draw the outline of a door, full-size, seven by three and a half.

"You see, Graham, there'll be four knobs. The lines between them will form a cross. And each knob will be connected to a set of wheels inside the door itself, and there will be four sets of hinges, one along each side but fixed only to the door, not to the frame." I shade these in. Graham cries. "A person will use the knob that will allow them to open the door in the direction they want—left or right, at their feet or above their heads. When a knob is turned it'll push the screws from the door into the hinges. People can open doors near windows without blocking morning or evening light, they'll carry furniture in and out with the door over their heads, never scraping its paint, and when they want to see the sky they can open it just a fraction at the top." On the wall I draw smaller diagrams of the door's different positions until the felt nib of the pen tatters. "It's a present to you, this door. I'm sorry it's not actual. You can imagine though how people might enjoy deciding how to walk through it. Patterns would form, families would have their habits."

"I wanted a father."

"Don't say that, Graham." He's crying still and I can't bear it.

"It's true."

I turn back to the desk and, kneeling there, scrawl a note. The pen is nearly ruined and it's hard to shape the letters. The writing takes time.

- Though some may accuse me of neglect, I have been consistent with the advice I always gave my children: never finish anything that bores you. Unfortunately, some of my children bored me. Graham never did. Please confirm this with him. He is the only one that meant anything to me.

"Graham," I say, crossing the room some minutes later to show him the piece of paper, to show him the truth.

He's lying on the bed, and as I stand over him I see that he's asleep. His tears have exhausted him. The skin about his closed eyes is puffy and red and from the corner of his mouth comes a rivulet of drool. I wipe it away with my thumb. I cup his gentle face in my hands and kiss him on the forehead.

From the other bed I take a blanket and cover him, pulling it up over his shoulders, tucking it beneath his chin. His breath is calm now, even. I leave the note folded by his side. I pat down his hair and turn off the lamp. It's time for me to go.

When I'm sure he's comfortable and sleeping soundly, I take my glass and the wine out into the hall. I can feel the weight of every step, my body beginning to tire. I lean against the wall, waiting for the elevator to take me down. The doors open and I enter.

From here in the descending glass cage I can see globes of orange light stretching along the boulevards of Santa Monica toward the beach where the shaded palms sway. I've always found the profusion of lights in American cities a cause for optimism, a sign of undiminished credulity, something to bear us along. In the distance, the shimmering pier juts into the vast darkness of the ocean like a burning ship launched into the night.

THE GOOD DOCTOR

AS HE PULLED up the drive, Frank saw the skeleton of a Chevy Nova, grass to the windows, rusting in the side yard like some battle-wasted tank. Toy guns and action figures, their plastic faded, lay scattered over the brown lawn. The house, a white fifties prefab, sagged to one side, the chimney tilting. To its left stood a dilapidated barn. From the green spray-painted letters on its door announcing *No Girls*

Allowed it seemed clear the building had some time ago been delivered from the intention of its creator into the hands of children.

He cut the engine and watched the cloud of dirt his tires had kicked up drift into a stand of oak trees shading the side of the house. They were the only trees in sight, empty prairie stretching miles in every direction. He rested his hands and chin over the top of the steering wheel, his head weighed down with the sinus ache of his hangover.

One of the reasons he'd taken his job at a county clinic two thousand miles from his friends and family was that the National Health Service Corps had promised to repay his medical school loans in return for three years' work in an underserved area. Last night he'd come back to his apartment to find a letter in the mail: Congress was cutting the program's funding, leaving him the full burden of his debt and a paltry salary to pay it with. He'd spent a year at the job already, and now they were hanging him out to dry. For the first time in his life there was uncertainty in his future. From college to medical school to residency to this job, everything had been applied for and planned. Now he wasn't even sure he could afford to stay. He'd got drunk on a bottle of scotch his friend from back East had sent him for his birthday. The last thing he had wanted to do today was drive two and half hours here to Ewing Falls to evaluate some woman who'd been refusing to visit the clinic for a year and demanding her medication by phone.

Nearly hundred-degree weather had settled over the state for the last week and today was no exception. With each step across the drive, more dirt rose powder dry into the air. By the time he mounted the porch steps, sweat dampened his collar.

A first knock produced no response. He waited a minute before tapping again. The shades in the front room were pulled to the middle of the windows and all he could see was the wood floor and the floral print back of a sofa. He turned to look across the yard and saw a girl standing in the driveway. She seemed to have appeared from nowhere. By the height of her, she looked eight or nine, but her rigid mouth and narrowed eyes suggested someone older.

"Hey, there." As soon as he spoke, the girl started walking quickly away, toward the trees.

"Hey," Frank called to her back, "are your folks home?"

"She ain't a bigger talker," a voice behind him said. Frank turned back toward the door to see a middle-aged man dressed in a sweatshirt and work pants. Spidery angiomas, those star-shaped discolorations of the vessels seen in liver patients, blotched the skin of his rounded face. Hepatitis C, Frank thought, or the end of a serious drinking habit. The man took a drag on his cigarette, holding the filter between thumb and forefinger, the exhaled smoke floating over the porch, tingling Frank's nostrils.

"You're the one they sent up from the clinic," he said flatly. He leaned forward, squinting. "Bit young to be a doctor, aren't you?"

Frank got this all the time: old ladies asking when the doctor would be in—a useful icebreaker, but he wasn't in the mood today.

"I'm here to see Mrs. Buckholdt," he said. "I assume she's home."

The man looked out across the fields, the horizon molten in air heated thick as the fumes of gasoline. The expression on his face changed from scrutiny to the more absent look of recollection, as though he had suddenly lost interest in their conversation.

"Yeah," he said, almost to himself. "She's in there."

Then he crossed the porch, past Frank, and wandered out into the yard.

"MRS. BUCKHOLDT?" FRANK called out, blinded momentarily by the darkness of the front hall.

"Down in a minute," she said, her voice coming from somewhere up beyond the stairwell.

Ahead in the kitchen, a cheetah chased a gazelle over the screen of a muted television. Frank could see the back of a boy's head silhouetted against the screen's lower half, the rest of him obscured by the counter. The house smelled of stale candy and the chemical salts of cheese-flavored snacks.

A bookcase stood on one side of the living room and a picture he couldn't make out in the poor light hung on the wall opposite. Two large Oriental carpets covered the floor. He put his briefcase down on a torn leather armchair and took out Mrs. Buckholdt's chart, which he would have read by now if he hadn't been in such poor shape this morning.

After getting thoroughly drunk, he'd done the really smart thing of calling his ex-girlfriend, a woman in his program he'd dated toward the end of their residency. They had gone out for six months, which, at the age of thirty-two, was the longest Frank had ever been with a woman. If he hadn't seen so many patients with romantic lives more desperate than his own, he might have considered himself abnormal. Anne had flown out from Boston a few times when he first got out here; he'd convinced himself that one day he would ask her to marry him.

"Glad to hear you're still out there saving the world," she said, after he made a few comments he regretted now. She knew he'd come out here with the idea that he'd be given the freedom to practice the way he wanted to, which meant more time to talk with his patients. Wanting such a thing seemed almost renegade at this point in his profession, given the dominance of the biological psychiatry they'd been trained in, a regime Anne had never seriously questioned. They'd argued about it plenty, always ending with her calling Frank a romantic clinging to an old myth about the value of talk. But no words of hers could change the fact that Frank had instincts about what it meant to spend time with the people he cared for, and they involved more than picking a drug. He knew his patients sought someone to acknowledge what they were experiencing, and he knew he was good at it, better than most of his colleagues.

At medical school, they all joked about the numbing: from four months spent dissecting the body of a dead man, cutting into his face and eyes, to seven hours clamping open a woman's chest, only to watch her expire on the table—whatever the particulars, it didn't take most people long. And then in residency, schizophrenics trembling in psychosis, addicts, manics, beaten children. Frank joked too. But he always felt odd doing it, as if it were a show to prove he was adapting like his peers. The fact was he still felt like a sponge, absorbing the pain of the people he listened to. Privately, he considered it the act of a certain kind of faith. Never having been a religious person, empathy had taken up the place in him belief might have in others.

Trying to ignore his headache, he skipped over the internist's report in Mrs. Buckholdt's chart and went straight to the psych note: forty-four-year-old woman with no history of major mental illness in the family; first presented with depression following death of her eldest son, four years ago; two younger children, boy and a girl. When he scanned the margin indicating course of treatment, he saw how shoddily her case had been managed. A brief course of antidepressants, probably never finished, and since then nothing but benzos—sedatives—written as needed. No therapy. George Pitford, the shrink Frank had replaced, wasn't about to drive five hours round-trip for a meds consult, so he'd just kept calling in her refills. A cryptic line he'd scrawled at the bottom of the page read, *Injury may be a factor.*

"My apologies for not greeting you at the door," Mrs. Buckholdt said, entering the living room, hands tucked in her pockets. She was an attractive woman, slender, taller than her husband, in better physical health, though she certainly looked older than forty-four. She wore tailored black pants, a bit faded, a white rayon shirt, a silver necklace. He'd been expecting a disorganized person, some kind of shut-in.

The woman before him seemed almost out of place here, in this house out in the middle of nowhere.

She closed the door to the kitchen, turned a key in the latch to lock it, then crossed the room to join him.

"I'm sorry you had to come all this way," she said. "In this awful heat. Would you like a drink? Water perhaps, or a lemonade?"

"I'm fine for now," he said, "thank you."

She took a seat on the couch and he lowered himself into the leather armchair.

"The reason I'm here is the director thought it would be a good idea for me to check in with you in person. He said you'd had some trouble getting down to the clinic for your last few appointments."

Her gaze rested somewhere over his shoulder. "I take it you're childless," she said.

Frank had patients who asked questions about his life, but they usually didn't come so fast.

"It might be best if we talked about how you've been doing lately. The clonazepam, it's an antianxiety drug. Have you been experiencing much anxiety lately?"

She lowered her glance momentarily to look Frank in the eye. She had a handsome, slightly gaunt face, powerful green eyes, a strong, almost male jawline; her black hair was brushed back off her high forehead. Frank didn't often see female patients with such a self-possessed demeanor. The women who came to him at the clinic usually had the blunt affect of beating victims or the long-untreated ill.

"You're here to write a prescription. Am I right?"

Frank was about to respond when Mrs. Buckholdt raised her left arm from her side to tuck a strand of hair behind her ear. As she did so, she lifted her other arm from her pocket to rest on her lap. All four digits were missing from her right hand, the skin grown smooth over the rounded ends of the knuckle bones. Frank couldn't help but stare at the fleshy little knobs. Some kind of farm accident, he guessed, the injury Pitford had mentioned. Catching himself, he focused resolutely on her face. Whatever he'd been planning to say had vanished from his mind.

"Maybe I'll have a glass of water after all," he said.

"Yes, do. Just help yourself. The key's in the door."

"HEY THERE," HE said to the boy in front of the television as he looked in the kitchen cupboard for a glass. Apparently this one wasn't a big talker either. He was slightly older than his sister, twelve perhaps. He stared at Frank with an odd expression, as if he were trying to decide if this man in front of him existed or was merely a passing mirage.

"What are you watching there?"

On the screen, a jackal or wolf fed on the gashed belly of a deer.

"You want some water?"

The boy shook his head.

THOUGH HE FELT odd doing it, Frank turned the key again in the door, locking it behind him as he reentered the living room. Mrs. Buckholdt hadn't moved from the couch. She sat rigid, her eyes following him as he crossed to his chair.

"I see you first visited the doctor about four years ago. That was just after your son died. The notes here say it was mostly depression you were coping with at that point. Is that right?"

"I wonder, Dr. Briggs. Where is it that you grew up?"

"Mrs. Buckholdt, I think that in the time we have it's important for me to get a handle on your situation so we can try to help you."

"Of course. I apologize. I just like having a sense of who I'm talking with. You're from the East I take it."

"Massachusetts."

"Whereabouts?"

"Outside Boston."

"I take it you grew up in a rich town."

"Mrs. Buckholdt—"

"I won't go on forever," she said. "But tell me, it's a rich town, isn't it? Tidy lawns. A country club. Kids going to college. Am I right?"

"A relatively affluent suburb, yes," he said, taken in by the gravity of her tone, chiding himself at once for being drawn out on a personal matter.

"Now, is the depression something you're still having an active problem with?" he asked firmly.

Her eyes wandered again over his shoulder, the same look of recollection he'd seen on her husband's face appearing now in hers. He realized she must be looking at the picture on the wall behind him. He turned to get a glimpse. It was a print of a late medieval painting, the image of a bustling town square during some kind of revel, all manner of people—vulgar, refined, youthful, decrepit—praying, eating, wandering through the square, the scene painted in browns and reds.

"It's a Brueghel," she said.

"Right," Frank replied, recognizing the name vaguely.

"*The Fight Between Carnival and Lent,* fifteen fifty-nine," she said. She examined Frank's expression, as if for signs of incredulity. "It may surprise you that I studied at one of your Eastern universities for a few years. My father liked to think of himself as a progressive man. Very liberal, always took his daughters seriously. He found pleasure in the fact I took up a thing as impractical as art history; used to drop it in conversation with friends at the Rotary and then chuckle in his way at their bemusement. He died while I was out there, just after I'd started my final year."

With her one good hand, she picked up a box of cigarettes, removed one, and lit it. Almost demurely, she blew the smoke down toward the floor.

"My mother wasn't so liberal. Spending all that money to look at pictures, for a girl, no less—what a waste, hey? So I came home—three years, no degree." She drew slowly on her cigarette. Her thoughts seemed to wander.

Though the shades were half pulled, the air in the front room was stifling. Frank could feel the back of his shirt dampening against the leather of the chair.

"I'm just wondering if maybe you could tell me a little about your symptoms."

"My symptoms?" she said, leaning forward. "Yes, I can tell you about my symptoms. Some mornings I wake up shaking, and I'm afraid to get out of my bed. If I take some of the pills I can manage to get up and make my children breakfast. Some mornings the fear's bad and I have to grit my teeth to get through it."

She rubbed her half-smoked cigarette out into the tarnished silver ashtray on the coffee table.

"And I'm afraid of my son."

"Why is that?"

Her already rigid body tightened a notch further. "Like I said, if I take the pills, it's fine."

Noticing her strained expression, Frank decided to back off. "You were saying you'd been to college. That's unusual for most of the women I see."

Mrs. Buckholdt leaned back in the couch and gave a small frown of acknowledgment, as if to say, yes, it was a pity more couldn't go. As she relaxed, a remnant of what must have once been coquettishness surfaced in her face, and Frank glimpsed how she must have looked to the other high school kids, the ones who'd never dreamt of leaving.

"My parents were good Lutherans. We'd always gone to this big, very plain barn of a church over in Long Pine, whitewash walls, a simple cross. My mother—when she came to visit me at college—those Gothic stone halls we lived in, she didn't like them, found them suspicious. There was something Catholic about gargoyles on the head of a drain; she didn't like the smell of it. She'd been happy with my father out here, couldn't imagine why a person would want to leave."

She gazed past Frank, through the window that looked out over the side yard.

"I'd always pictured heaven as a rather ordinary place, where you met the dead and people were more or less comfortable. I think I imagined the whole world that way, as an ordinary place. But those paintings . . . they were so beautiful. I'd never seen anything so perfect in my life. Do you know Géricault? Do you know his pictures of Arcadia, those huge, lush landscapes of his?"

Frank shook his head.

"You should see them someday. They're beautiful things to see." She spoke in a slow, reflective manner.

"You came home, then," he asked, "when you left college?"

"Yes, to my parents' house." She smiled. "Jack was just starting as an officer down at the bank. He'd spent a year at the state university, read a good deal. He didn't want to stay here forever. Kept telling me that, because he knew it had been hard for me—coming back. He'd drive me out to the lake in his convertible. And he'd talk about a house in a town out in California. Always California. An orange tree in the backyard, how you could drive with the roof down all year round, a porch with a view of the ocean. I kept thinking of being close to a museum. I could enroll in classes again; it wouldn't have taken many to finish. And near a city, I might do research. Jack—he'd nod at that. I was a college girl, you see, a catch." She chuckled. "Twenty-five years ago, that ghost you saw out there—he was a handsome boy." Her eyes came to rest on the floor by her feet. "Are you married, Dr. Briggs?"

There was a familiarity, almost a caring, to the way she asked the question, as though she were inquiring not for her own information but to give him the chance to tell her.

"No," he said. "I'm not."

"Is it something you hope to do?"

He imagined his professors judging him unprofessional for answering these questions. "Yes," he said, "I'd like to."

She nodded but made no reply.

"You married soon after you returned?" he asked.

"That's right. Jason, my first son, he came early on. Of course, it made sense to save money for a while. Get a house here, just for a year or two, before the big move. I imagine you went to a Montessori, didn't you? Or a country day school—maps on the walls." She smiled at Frank, a wan, generous smile. "He was so bright, Doctor, from the very beginning. I *wanted* him to have all that. I really did.

"I'd kept my books from college, and there were the ones Jack had, and some I bought. So while the school taught him George Washington every year, I read to him. I wasn't a fanatic, I didn't throw the television out, we didn't ground him. I read him books after supper and when he got older he read them himself. And I showed him things. I played him records, drove him to Chicago once, took him to the museum. He liked the paintings all right, but you should have seen the look on his face when he saw the height of those buildings and all the people in the streets—delighted, that's what he was, delighted. I couldn't stand the idea of him hanging around here, waiting for some dead-end job. Of course that made me a snob, wanting more for him. Those teachers down at the high school, they didn't like me. Too much trouble.

"Round about when he was fourteen, this place, it started doing its work on him somehow. I could see it happening. The little tough guy stance, afraid of anything that wouldn't make him popular. His father had started drinking by then. Everything was going to hell around here, prices dropping through the floor, all these farms that couldn't make a dime. Jack spent his days taking people's homes and property their families had owned for decades. So it didn't worry me at first, I figured the man deserved a drink or two when he came home. That was before the bank went under. And as for symptoms, yes, to tell you the truth, I was depressed. I was. Things hadn't gone like we'd planned. I kept thinking about the girls I'd roomed with, visiting Europe, standing in front of those pictures. I shouldn't have done that—let myself look back that way. It's the sort of thing kids notice, the way you're not really there in the room with them."

She paused. It appeared to Frank as though she were deciding whether or not to go on. Their eyes met briefly, but he said nothing.

"There was a kid," she said, eventually. "Jimmy Green. His parents had lost their house; the family was living with relatives out on Valentine. He and Jason started spending their time together. He rode an old motorcycle and they'd be out in that barn with it for hours, doing I don't know what, fixing it, I guess. Since he was eight, I'd driven Jason over to Tilden for violin lessons. He'd gotten some grief for it at school, kids calling him names. He'd cried about it some when he was younger, but he loved that music. Used to sit in that wicker chair right over there by the door, his little legs bouncing, twenty minutes before we even got in the car, his eyes begging me to hurry. You know he stood in this room one evening after practice and played five minutes of Mozart for his younger brother and sister? *Mozart.* Can you believe that? In *this* living room." She shook her head, amazed.

"About a year after he started hanging around the Green boy, I was sitting in the drive waiting for him to come out—he'd spent all day in that barn, we were late. Before he left the porch, he took his instrument out of the case."

Her jaw tightened, her lips barely moving.

"We'd bought the violin together. Years ago, on a trip to Saint Louis. His father had given him the money and he'd stood on his toes to hand it to the salesman. That day I was waiting in the car to take him to his lesson, he walked up and smashed his violin on the hood. Said he was tired, didn't feel like going that afternoon. That's what he said: tired. Just like that. Walked back into the barn."

In her voice, there was only the blankness of reporting. Not a trace of sorrow.

"You're a doctor in these parts," she said. "You must know all about methamphetamine."

Frank nodded. He'd seen some of it in the clinic, and heard more. It had become the drug of choice for kids out here, cheaper than coke and without the hippie connotations of pot. In the end, it wasn't the drug itself that got people but the lack of sleep it caused. After three or four days of no rest the body collapsed or slipped into psychosis.

"I told his father he had to do something, had to go to the Greens, or down to the school, find out who they were getting it from. But Jack—he didn't have it in him. The bank had been shut three years, he was scared of everything by then.

"I suppose I should have put Jason in the car and driven him out of here, gone with him somewhere. I didn't, though. I just took it from him whenever I could. I searched his room every day for those little envelopes of crystals. I checked the pockets of his trousers, begged him to stop. You know, once I even told him I'd buy him marijuana instead. His own mother. When the police finally caught the two of them buying it in the parking lot down by the market, I was glad. I thought it would shake him up. He spent three months up at Atkinson, at the juvenile center." She caught Frank's look. "You think that was a mistake."

"It's a rough place, but it was out of your hands."

"Well, you're right. It didn't help. He was worse when he got back, angrier, more confused. And he still did it. I don't think he even stopped while he was in there—how that can be, how they can run a jail where children can get drugs, I just don't know how that can be . . . and of course he was so young, just sixteen, boys at that age—" She broke off. "All those hormones in him . . . I suppose the drug—" She stopped again, covering her mouth with her hand.

"I was here, in the living room. It was a Sunday. Jack had taken the kids over to visit his sister. Jason had been so erratic those last few days, we were trying to keep the younger ones away from him. He'd been out till dawn that morning and the morning before and then up there in his room all day, but not sleeping, I could tell he wasn't sleeping. I was waiting for him to come down to eat something. I kept thinking, just one more conversation, we'd talk and somehow . . .

"I was right here on the couch. I heard his door open, and then I heard him crying. It was like years ago when he was a boy and he'd had an upset at school and I'd sit with him out there on the porch with his head in my lap as the sun went down and I'd tell him how one day we'd take a trip on a boat all the way across the Atlantic and he'd see Athens and Rome and all the places where the stories I'd read him took place, and he'd fall asleep listening to me. When I heard him cry that day I thought maybe it was all over—that he had come back to me somehow. He hadn't cried in so long. I went up the stairs.

"My son. He was naked. He'd been rubbing himself. For hours, it must have been. He'd rubbed himself raw. He was bleeding down there. And he was crying, his tears catching in the little beard that had started growing on his cheeks, the soft little brown hairs he hadn't learned to shave yet. When I got to the top of the stairs he looked at me like I'd severed a rope he'd been clinging to for dear life, just like that, like I'd sent him down somewhere to die. What could I do?

"I got a towel. From the bathroom. A white towel. I got gauze and ointment, and I sat him down on his bed and I cleaned him and put Band-Aids on him and I tried not to weep."

Mrs. Buckholdt sat on the edge of the sofa, shoulders

hunched forward. Her words had drained her, her face gone pale now. She stared blankly at the floor.

"I was his mother," she said quietly, almost listlessly. "What was I supposed to do?"

For a moment, there was silence in the room.

"The kitchen," she said. "I was in the kitchen. Later. Making him soup. He'd always liked soup. Maybe he'd taken the drug again. I don't know. I felt him behind me. Suddenly he grabbed my wrist, forced it down onto the cutting board, and he chopped my fingers off, the fingers I'd touched him with, chopped them off with a meat cleaver. Then he walked out naked into the backyard."

THE TWO OF them sat there together a long time, the sun hanging low on the rim of the western sky, casting its giant columns of light down over the land, level over the yard, level through the unshaded panes of the windows, pouring over Mrs. Buckholdt's back, casting shadow over the coffee table and the tarnished ashtray and the rounded, dark center of the densely patterned wool carpet.

In the time she had spoken, it seemed to Frank as if Mrs. Buckholdt's body had sunk down into itself, leaving her smaller and more frail, her earlier, imposing demeanor exhausted. He experienced a familiar comfort being in the presence of another person's unknowable pain. More than any landscape, this place felt like home.

"How did your son die?" he asked.

"The two of them, he and Jimmy, they'd borrowed some

friend's truck. It was only a few days later—he never had come back to the house. They were out on the interstate, headed west. They crashed into the wall of an overpass. Jimmy made it with some burns. He still lives out there on Valentine. I see him now and again."

By dint of habit, the trained portion of Frank's mind composed a note for Mrs. Buckholdt's chart: Patient actively relives a traumatic event with intrusive recall; there are depressive features, hypervigilance, and generalized anxiety. Diagnosis: posttraumatic stress disorder. Treatment: a course of sertraline, one hundred milligrams daily, recommendation for psychotherapy, eventual titration off clonazepam.

He wondered how his colleagues felt when they said these words to themselves or wrote them on a piece of paper. Did the power to describe the people they listened to save them from what they heard? Did it absolve them of their duty to care?

As the silence between them stretched out, Frank remembered the first patient he'd seen as a resident, a woman whose husband had died in a plane crash. Each hour they spent together she filled with news of her two children, her son's play at school, a job her daughter had taken at a hotel, right down to what they had chosen to wear that morning, and she said it all gazing out the window, as though she were describing events in the history of a foreign country.

He could remember lying in bed on the nights after he'd seen her, alone in his apartment, her plight weighing on him like a congregant's soul on the spirit of a minister or a character's fate on the mind and body of a writer. Often, lying there, he would remember an earlier night, lying in his bed as a child, soon after his family had moved to a new town. Their house was still full of boxes, and their parents had been arguing. From the other bedroom, he heard his older brother talking to their mother in a scared tone: he hated his new school, the unfamiliar kids, the way they pushed him around, and he wanted so very badly not to go back in the morning. The fear in his voice troubled the air like an alarm. Their mother's voice was lower, her reassurances muffled by the distance of the hall. Frank had wept himself to sleep, pained to tears that he could do nothing to prevent his brother's suffering.

He thought now how it had always been for him, ever since he was a boy sitting on the edge of a chair in the living room listening to his parents' friends—a divorced woman whose hands shook slightly in her lap as she told him with great excitement about the vacation she was to take, or the man whose son Frank saw teased relentlessly at school, talking of how happy his boy was—the unsaid visible in their gestures, filling the air around them, pressing on Frank. And later in college, at a party, drink in hand, standing by a bookcase, chatting with a slightly heavy girl hanging back from the crowd, tracked into every shift of her eyes, every tense little smile, as if the nerves in her body were the nerves in his, her every attempt to disguise her awkwardness raising its pitch in him.

Sitting in front of this oddly compelling woman, he realized more clearly than ever before this was why he'd become a doctor: to organize his involuntary proximity to human pain. He could use his excuse of debt to leave his position at the clinic; he could even leave his profession, move away, anywhere, but still there would be this opening in him.

Mrs. Buckholdt rose from the couch and stood by the window. As she raised the shade, more of the waning sun flooded the room. Her shoulders tensed at the sound of a knock on the other side of the kitchen door. Frank watched her take a breath.

"What is it, darling?" she called out.

"Can I come in?" a quiet voice asked.

She crossed to unlock the door. The boy edged his way into the room. Biting her lower lip, holding herself rigid, Mrs. Buckholdt managed to run her hand through her son's hair.

"What is it, dear?"

"When are we leaving?"

"In a few minutes," she said. "Go ahead and get ready."

The boy stared for a moment at Frank, his expression as mysterious as before. He turned back into the kitchen and they listened to his steps as he climbed the back stairs.

"Mrs. Buckholdt," Frank began, knowing that by saying what he was about to say he was committing himself to remaining here, to finding some way to scrape by. People like this woman needed him, needed a person to listen. "In situations like yours, it can help a great deal if you have someone to talk with. I couldn't see you every week, but I could do it once a month, and if you were able perhaps to get down to my office, we might meet once every two weeks. We could sign you up for free care. The drugs can only do so much."

She had remained standing by the door, her arms crossed over her chest. "That's generous of you," she said, taking a step into the center of the room.

After a moment's pause, she looked again at the picture on the wall. "That print there," she said, "it was his favorite. He picked it out at the museum in Chicago. He loved all the different characters, the bits of activity."

Frank turned to look. In the left foreground, a tavern overflowed with townspeople, drinkers spilling into the street, following in the wake of a large-bellied mandolin player wearing a floppy hat. In front of him, the obese leader of the carnival sat, as if on horseback, astride a massive wine barrel pushed forward by the revelers, his lance a spit of meat. Opposite him and his train, somberly dressed people stood praying in some rough formation behind a gaunt, pale man propped up in a chair—Lent holding out before him a baker's pole. He faced the leader of the carnival band, the two posed in mock battle. Behind these contending forces, the square bustled. Fishwives gutting their fish on a wooden block, boys playing at a stick and tethered ball, dancers dancing, merchants selling, children peering from windows, a woman on a ladder scrubbing the walls of a house. There were cripples missing limbs, almsmen begging by the well. A man and woman made love. Another couple, dressed in Puritan costume, their backs to the viewer, were led by a fool through the middle of it all.

"Certainly no Arcadia," she said. "Nothing lush about it, not the kind of painting I fell in love with. I've looked at it a lot since he's been gone. My professors taught me Brueghel was a moralizer, his paintings full of parables. But that's not what I see anymore. I just see how *much* there is, how much life."

She looked at Frank. "The woman over in Tilden, she teaches Michael the violin now, and she won't let me pay her. He's not as good as his brother was, but he's good."

She bowed her head. "You seem like a kind man, and you're kind to offer what you did. But I don't want you to come back here. And I don't want to come to your office. A few days a week I use those pills to get by, but there are days when I manage without them. Those are the better days. When I don't look back, when I'm not afraid—better for my kids too. If you feel like you can't write me a prescription, I understand. I'll survive without it."

The boy could be heard at the top of the front stairs. Frank rose from his chair and took a step toward Mrs. Buckholdt. She turned to watch her son enter the room, carrying his violin case. Quietly, he took a seat in the wicker chair by the door.

"Go and get your father," she said. "Tell him it's time to leave." He ran along the hall, into the kitchen, and out the back door.

Frank's stomach tightened, the panic beginning before his mind could form the thought: he didn't want to lose her, he didn't want the telling to end.

Mrs. Buckholdt took her handbag from the front table.

"It really is recommended in almost all cases such as this that a patient undergo some kind of therapy, and given the extremity—"

"Dr. Briggs," she interrupted, opening the front door to the view out over the yard and beyond to the empty road, "didn't you hear what I said?"

THE BEGINNINGS OF GRIEF

A YEAR AFTER my mother's suicide I broke a promise to myself not to burden my father with worries of my own. I told him how unhappy I was at school, how lonely I felt. From the wing chair where he crouched in the evenings he asked, "What can I do?" The following afternoon, coming home from work the back way, he missed a stop sign. A van full of sheet glass going forty miles an hour hit the driver's side of the

Taurus. According to the policeman who knocked on the front door in tears, my father died with the first shattering impact. An aunt from Little Rock stayed for a week, cooking stews and Danish pastry. She said I could come and live with her in Arkansas. I told her I didn't want to. As I had only a year and a half left of high school, we decided I could finish up where I was, and she arranged for me to live with a neighbor.

Mrs. Polk was sixty, her mother eighty-five. They had between them a closet of fourteen blue flowered dresses, which the maid laundered on Tuesdays. They watched a considerable amount of public television and spoke in hushed tones of relatives in Pittsburgh. I was given dead Mr. Polk's study with a cot in the corner. The ladies paid no attention to my coming and going and I spent as little time at their house as I could.

In industrial arts that fall, Mr. Raffello gave us a choice of projects: bookcase, spice rack, or a chest about the size of a child's coffin. I picked the last of these, and because we had to pay for our own wood, I used pine. I took exact measurements and sanded each board with three grades of paper. All the equipment was there in the shop: hammers and vises, finishing nails and glue, planers and table saws. The machines had shiny metal casings and made a deafening roar. If I had been allowed to, I would've stayed all day.

I found the class entrancing for another reason: the chance to be with Gramm Slater, an angry, cherub-faced boy who wore steel-tip boots and a baseball cap pulled over his brow. He stood a head above the other kids, already as large framed as my father, his forearms covered in a layer of golden hair. His lips curled easily into a sneer and his eyes were full of mockery. When he caught me gazing at him, he'd smirk knowingly, like an angel. Twice our shoulders had touched in the cafeteria line.

On a Friday afternoon a few weeks after my father died, Mr. Raffello began explaining the use of clamps. The thermos of gin I'd washed my sloppy joe down with at lunch made concentration a challenge but like a good student, I held on to my bench and remained upright. It struck me our teacher might be an inhabitant of some kingdom of middle earth, with his rickety frame and nose jutting over his mouth like a cliff above the entrance of a cave. His voice sounded like the bass notes of an organ.

"The instrument is here in your hand. You've sanded your wood. You've applied your glue. The time for the clamp has arrived."

Eyes in the class fluttered shut as his bony hands began turning the rod. Steel squeaked in the thread. I imagined the sound as the creaking of a ferry's oar in its lock as we pulled away from the shore.

Leaning into the noise, I watched Gramm on the stool beside me. He sat hunched forward. Through his worn cotton T-shirt, I traced the perfect arch of his spine. I wanted him to look at me. I wanted him to touch me. I didn't care how.

My foot reached out and tapped him on the shin.

"What the fuck?" he whispered, his sneer coming to life.

I suppose the incident could have ended there, but the expression on his face, the way his eyes narrowed and his upper lip flared off his front teeth, appeared to me so beautiful I couldn't stand to see it fade. I swung my foot back and hammered him on the calf. This brought a wonderful color to his cheeks.

"Cut the shit!" he said in a louder whisper, turning the heads of our neighboring carpenters. The sound had traveled up to the front of the industrial arts studio, where Mr. Raffello cast his ancient eye to us and said, "If you never learn to clamp, you never learn to build."

I swung again, nailing Gramm in the ankle. He jumped off his stool and I thought he'd punch me right then, but instead he paused. The scraping of the other students' chairs filled the room. If there was a fight we both knew he'd win. I sensed the amazement in him at what he was about to do, the sheer pleasure of an excuse for rage. At last it came, his fist planted just under my heart like a battering ram against the gates of a castle. The air rushed from my lungs and I fell backward onto a low bench. Looking up, I saw him closing on me. My muscles went limp. I waited for his tackle.

But Mr. Raffello had reached Gramm by then and he stepped between us.

GRAMM STARTED CALLING me faggot and dissed me in front of my classmates, who were appalled he could do such a thing to someone who everyone knew had lost both his parents in a year. Most people thought silence was kindest. But whenever he and I saw each other on our street or at the supermarket where I bagged groceries, he showed a sullen kind of interest in me.

On a Saturday in the beginning of March, he came in the store to buy orange juice and asked me what I was doing that night. I told him nothing, and he laughed. He said if I didn't want to be a loser my whole life I should come to his house, where he planned to get drunk.

I arrived at about ten o'clock, expecting a party. As it turned out, Gramm was alone. His eyes were bloodshot and he smelled of dope. He offered me a vodka and orange as soon as we got into the kitchen.

"Where's your mom?" I asked.

"She went shopping somewhere for the weekend."

Mrs. Slater had been divorced three times and was very rich as a result of it. The house had six bedrooms and was built in the style of an old Southern mansion. Small computer screens embedded in the walls controlled every appliance and light.

"Nice place," I said.

"It's all right."

On the counter, a tabby cat picked at a mound of smoked salmon. Gramm spooned a blue-black paste of tiny eggs onto another plate and pushed it under the animal's nose. The cat sniffed the new offering and returned to the fish.

"I had a snake," Gramm said. "It died from some skin disease. The vet told us to put it in a garbage can full of rocks and cold water but it still died. I think the vet was wrong. I think the vet's a fucking idiot."

"Sounds like it."

"You want to get high?"

"Sure," I nodded, savoring the damp touch of his fingertips as he passed the joint.

"Why did you come over here?" he asked.

"You invited me."

He laughed, as though that were no reason at all.

I swallowed my drink whole and poured another vodka.

"How come you kicked me in Raffello's class?"

"I was just kidding around."

"Bullshit."

"Is anybody else coming over?"

"Why? Are you afraid?"

I knew I should fire back something like "Afraid of what?"—that this would be the proper, male thing to do. Yet we both seemed to know the futility of such a gesture and I couldn't bring myself to pretend.

Gramm slouched in a chair between me and the sink. As I passed by him to put my glass on the counter, he stuck his foot out and tripped me. I hit the tile floor with my shoulder; the glass fell from my hand and shattered by the door of the fridge. I rolled onto my back and saw the same giddy expression on Gramm's face he'd flashed the day I first got his attention. My heart thumped against my rib cage like a ball dribbled close to the pavement.

"Aren't you going to get up?" he asked sarcastically, understanding already that I wouldn't, that he'd have to lift me from the floor. The knowledge seemed to anger him. He drew his leg back and kicked me in the thigh. I let out a moan of relief as the pain shot up my spine.

"There you go, cocksucker. How was that?"

He lifted his glass to his mouth, the bottom of his T-shirt rose from the waist of his jeans, and I could see the smattering of light brown hair around his belly button. I wanted to run my tongue over it. More than anything in the world.

He took a step forward and pressed the sole of his shoe lightly against my cheek. "I could squash you like a bug," he said. He wasn't the most articulate boy I ever met. Only the one whose pain seemed to me most beautiful. I reached out and grabbed his ankle but he tore his leg away at once and kicked me hard in the stomach, jamming me against the cabinet door. Air rushed from my lungs and I slumped facedown on the linoleum. All of a sudden, I felt very tired. He kicked me several times more, but the blows seemed to come from farther away.

When he dragged me out of the kitchen, I opened my eyes, strained my head up, but my vision blurred and I could only see the outline of him.

In the bedroom, he kept the lights off and if I made any sound at all, he stung my cheek with the palm of his hand. When I reached up to caress his bare chest, he punched me so hard in the shoulder I thought he'd broken the bone. I learned quickly just how this thing would work.

THE FIRST FEW notes I put through the grate of his locker that next week went unanswered. In the halls, Gramm ignored me now rather than harassing me. He'd give a nervous glance as I passed him and his circle of friends smoking cigarettes in the courtyard. The bruises he'd given me were concealed beneath my shirt; I'd run my hands over the swollen flesh and think of him. Sometimes I'd get sufficiently drunk at lunch that an hour would pass and I'd realize all I'd done was stand across the hall from his classroom, gazing at the back of his head, imagining my fingers brushing his soft hair.

I didn't go to my own classes much anymore. Mr. Farb, the school shrink, would find me in the cafeteria and walk me to his office, where he'd talk sincerely about the five stages of grief. A short, bearded man, he wore diamond-check cardigans and a thick wedding ring. When he rocked back in his chair, his feet dangled like a child's.

"How's the college search going?" he asked once.

"The college search? It's going great. I'm applying to Princeton."

"Really?"

"Yeah, and Harvard too."

"Impressive."

"And the University of Beijing."

"Oh," he said. "That's . . . ambitious. And your new home environment, is it supportive?"

"The maid gives me crucifixes."

He rotated his wedding ring about his hairy knuckle and asked me if there was anyone *special* at the moment, and I decided he wasn't ready to hear about my life. When he asked how I felt, I said fine. This seemed to relieve him and he wrote notes for all my absences.

At last, I got a crumpled bit of paper at the bottom of my locker saying Gramm would be alone at his house on a Friday afternoon. I left school early that day and walked the two miles to his house. When I rang the doorbell there was no answer and I sat for an hour on the front lawn before I saw Gramm coming up the hill. He spotted me from a hundred yards and slowed his pace. When he reached the driveway he gave a nod and then stood mute for a minute or two, glancing from the tarmac to the house to me. He looked tired and nervous. When he headed for the back door, I followed him inside.

In the kitchen, Gramm hesitated by the sink and from the way he hunched over it, I thought he might be sick to his stomach.

"What's the matter?" I asked.

"Why did you come?" His voice had no sarcasm in it now. The question plagued him.

"I got your note," I said softly, knowingly, the way I imagined a lover would speak of such things.

He bowed his head, shamed by the memory, and as I saw his cheeks redden I felt a pity for him so overwhelming it brought tears to my eyes. I crossed the room and laid a hand gently on his shoulder. His body convulsed as though my fingers were the live ends of a power cord. He jerked from under my touch, reaching back to swat away my arm. I stepped forward again and placed a hand on his chest.

"Don't touch me!" he shouted.

I ran my fingers through his golden hair.

His fist smashed into my stomach and I grabbed at his

upper arm with both hands but he shook himself free and pushed me onto the floor. I rolled onto my belly and lay silent, my erection throbbing against the hard tiles.

With my eyes closed, I imagined him as a gladiator, wearing breastplate and shield, the sun warming his full shoulders, the crowd cheering him on. With a nod of the head, the emperor tells his champion to give the people what they want. I smell the bronzed skin of his ankle, listen to the masses roar.

Behind me, the cupboard opened and I heard his lips on the mouth of a bottle.

"Get up," he said.

I made no response, and he yelled again—"Get up!"—kicking me in the flank. But I held my ground.

Twice more the force of his shoe nearly lifted me off the floor, stripping my mind of everything but this lucid pain. His voice filled the void.

"Garbage," he whispered. "You're garbage."

He crouched over me and using both hands yanked my pants down from my waist. Standing, he pressed the toe of his shoe between my legs. "My father says people like you are sick. You've got some kind of moral sickness. Like you want to be a woman but you're just a weak, puny shit of a boy and everything your sick mind wants is dirt."

He removed his shoe from between the cheeks of my ass and kicked me there, forcing water into my eyes. But I made no sound.

"Talk to me, you little fuck!" he shouted.

Something heavy and sharp edged struck my back and I

couldn't help letting out a groan. Across the kitchen floor, the tabby cat stared.

I heard Gramm take up the bottle again and leave the room.

For some time, I lay quiet. My side ached and I could feel blood leaking from the cut. The sound of television echoed in the other room. I got up and stepping out of my crumpled pants walked half naked into the den. On the TV screen, cops pinned down a Latino man who was yelling something as a group of small children wailed on the shoulder of a freeway. The shuddering of a helicopter's wings muffled the voices. A giant recliner faced the TV. As I walked closer I saw the top of Gramm's head over its back, his legs stretched onto the footrest. He lifted his bottle to his mouth and swallowed.

I walked around to stand between him and the television. His mouth hung slightly open as he gazed at my body, stripped from the waist down.

"You must want to die," he said.

He stepped out of the chair. I closed my eyes. This must have been a fresh insult to him, for as soon as he reached me he slapped me across the face. Once the first blow came, the rest followed in a hail, knuckles to my temple and cheek, a knee against my chest. I fell to one side, collapsing onto the carpet. My mind drifted as I heard him pull down his jeans and then I felt his warm flesh against my back as he crawled on top of me, spreading my legs with his knees. The children's keening rose above the beating of the chopper's wings and the roar of the crowd in my head. Furiously, he stabbed me, again and again.

"WHAT ON EARTH have you been doing?" Mrs. Polk asked when I stepped into the living room. "Watch out! You'll get blood on the carpet."

Her mother hauled her attention from the television and shouted, "WHO'S THIS!"

"THE BOY!" Mrs. Polk yelled back. "THE BOY! The one who lives with us."

"OH!" her mother shouted before raising the volume. A couple in riding gear cantered over the lawn of a manor house. I leaned against the door and fainted.

NATALIA, THE MAID, drove me to the emergency room, where they washed the blood from my face and thighs. A nurse in her twenties, wearing lozenge-shaped silver earrings like the ones my mother had on when I lifted her head from the oven to rest on my lap, asked me lots of questions about where I had been and what had happened. I told her I was walking home from school when a guy in a van full of sheet glass offered me a ride; he brought me to a clearing in the woods, I said. They took X rays and told me there was no permanent damage. The nurse said I should come back and talk to someone at the hospital but I told her I already had a shrink. Natalia gave me a crucifix and begged me to wear it around my neck.

At school, most people were too afraid to ask what had happened, except the lady in the office, who wept when I gave her the doctor's note. A mugging in the city, it said.

The few times I saw Gramm, he walked quickly in the other direction. He stopped coming to Mr. Raffello's class, which for me was the only place I felt any sense of purpose.

I gave my pine chest another sanding with the finest grade of paper, smoothing every sharp corner and point. With a cloth, I applied the first coat of stain, a dark, amber brown that brought out the grain of the wood nicely. When it was dry I put on another coat, and over that a shiny polyurethane finish. To complete the design, I chose a brass lock from the hardware and affixed it to the lid.

Mr. Raffello went around the classroom examining students' work. When he reached my bench, his eyes wandered my face, reading the marks and bruises like a story he'd heard a hundred times before.

"Who hit you?" he asked.

I stared at the hem of his black shop coat, imagined it as a ferryman's cape. Maybe he'd think my tale unremarkable, having known so many. Maybe he'd listen in comprehending silence as he rowed me across.

"Nobody," I said.

"What are you going to do with the chest?"

I pictured myself curled inside it.

"I don't know," I said.

"Well, you've done a good job," he muttered. "Put your address on it. I'll drop it off next week."

I'D KEPT A set of keys to my parents' house and as the real estate lady hadn't found a buyer yet, the place was empty. I'd go in the afternoons to sit in my room, where the water glass still waited on the bedside table and the clock radio faithfully kept time. From the window, where I watched for Gramm, I heard my father turning the pages of his newspaper, my mother whispering; the sounds floated in the hallway just outside my door. The house was rotting.

I'd left just one note in Gramm's locker, telling him that I came here after school, asking him to visit. For days after that, I didn't see him. Someone mentioned he was sick and had been missing soccer practice. Still, I went to my house and waited.

He came on a Tuesday. Rain was falling through the naked branches of the trees onto a carpet of rotting foliage. Gramm paused in front of the house, his hands buried in his pockets, the hood of his sweatshirt sheltering him from the weather. For several minutes he stood there, glancing back in the direction from which he'd come and then again at the gray shutters and curtained windows.

He was shaking when I opened the door. I led him into the kitchen.

"Are you sick?" I asked.

He shrugged. Under the room's overhead light, he looked pale, worn out, the mockery all gone. I offered him a drink but he shook his head. He was upset. I poured him a vodka anyway and put it down beside him.

"Listen," he said suddenly. "I'm sorry about what happened to your parents." He spoke in a rush, as though he'd been holding the sentiment in for days and needed to be rid of it.

I tightened my grip on the counter's sharp edge until I felt nothing but pain radiating from the palm of my hand.

"I just think we should forget about all this," he said. "Can we do that? Can we forget about it?"

I said nothing.

His shoulders quivered.

"Why did you ask me here?" he said, the resolve drained from his voice.

"I wanted to see you."

"Don't say that."

"It's true."

I crossed to where he sat, and taking his right hand in mine, moved it to the table, wrapping his damp fingers around the glass. He held his breath as I touched him.

"Drink it," I said.

With shaking hand, he lifted the glass to his lips. I watched the lump of his throat rise and fall as he swallowed. When he'd finished, I filled the glass again.

"Go on," I said.

He shook his head.

"Go on," I repeated. "I want you to."

He obeyed, emptying the glass twice more as I stood over him. I put the bottle down and lifted my T-shirt off, baring the purple and yellowed bruises that covered my chest. He shrunk back, closing his eyes. With my thumbs, I pressed them open again. I knelt before him. I took hold of his loose hands and formed them into fists. He wept. The tears ran down his pale cheeks and dripped from his chin.

"Please," he whispered, "let me go."

I slid my fingers along the inside of his thigh. Through his cotton pants, I cupped his balls gently in my hand. I felt his penis swell, his muscles tense. He drew back the fist I had made for him and hit me in the eye, sobbing as he did it.

"Are you happy now?" he cried.

"No," I said.

He swung again and knocked me against the door of the oven. Beneath the tears I saw blood in his cheeks, glow of the boy I'd spent years admiring. I lifted myself to my knees and from the drawer by the stove I took the knife my father used to cut tomatoes and onions on the nights he'd tried to make me dinner, crying as he boiled water in my mother's pots. I offered the knife up to Gramm and when he would not take it I put it in his hand and closed his fingers over the handle. Leaning forward, I hugged him around the legs, burying my face in the warmth of his stomach.

Waiting. Hoping.

WE REMAINED TOUCHING like that for several minutes, the rise and fall of his belly against my cheek the only movement. His weeping stopped, and gradually his breath became deep and even. He placed the blade on the counter over my shoulder and then gently backed away.

It felt as though a long time had passed, as though we had been traveling some great distance and were now tired, sapped of the force that had brought us here, empty, to this room. I knew a sudden shame at the sight of my bruised skin and stood up to put on my shirt. At the table, Gramm sat motionless, his unblinking eyes turned finally inward.

I moved to the window. Outside, the rain had tapered to a drizzle. Weeds in my mother's garden, bent low by the earlier downpour, swayed now in the breeze. On the branches of the dogwood, crows shook their black feathers.

As I watched the storm passing, a pickup slowed across the street in front of Mrs. Polk's house and pulled into her drive. Mr. Raffello stepped around the bed of the truck, and lifting the plastic sheeting, raised my dark amber chest in his arms.

For the first time in a long while, I began to cry.

DEVOTION

THROUGH THE OPEN French doors, Owen surveyed the garden. The day was hot for June, a pale sun burning in a cloudless sky, wilting the last of the irises, the rhododendron blossoms drooping. A breeze moved through the laburnum trees, carrying a sheet of the Sunday paper into the rose border. Mrs. Giles's collie yapped on the other side of the hedge.

With his handkerchief, Owen wiped sweat from the back of his neck.

His sister, Hillary, stood at the counter sorting strawberries. She'd nearly finished the dinner preparations, though Ben wouldn't arrive for hours yet. She wore a beige linen dress he'd never seen on her before. Her black-and-gray hair, usually kept up in a bun, hung down to her shoulders. For a woman in her mid-fifties, she had a slender, graceful figure.

"You're awfully dressed up," he said.

"The wine," she said. "Why don't you open a bottle of the red? And we'll need the tray from the dining room."

"We're using the silver, are we?"

"Yes, I thought we would."

"We didn't use the silver at Christmas."

He watched Hillary dig for something in the fridge.

"It should be on the right under the carving dish," she said.

Raising himself from his chair, Owen walked through into the dining room. From the sideboard he removed the familiar gravy boats and serving dishes until he found the tarnished platter. The china and silver had come from their parents' when their father died, along with the side tables and sitting chairs and the pictures on the walls.

"It'd take an hour to clean this," he called into the kitchen.

"There's polish in the cabinet."

"We've *five* perfectly good trays in the cupboard."

"It's behind the drink, on the left."

He gritted his teeth. She could be so bloody imperious.

"This is some production," he muttered, seated again at

the kitchen table. He daubed a cloth in polish and drew it over the smooth metal. They weren't in the habit of having people in to dinner. Aunt Philippa from Shropshire, their mother's sister, usually came at Christmas and stayed three or four nights. Now and again, Hillary had Miriam Franks, one of her fellow teachers from the comprehensive, in on a Sunday. They'd have coffee in the living room afterward and talk about the students. Occasionally they'd go out if a new restaurant opened on the High Street, but they'd never been gourmets. Most of Owen's partners at the firm had professed to discover wine at a certain age and now took their holidays in Italy. He and Hillary rented a cottage in the Lake District the last two weeks of August. They had been going for years and were perfectly happy with it. A nice little stone house that caught all the afternoon light and had a view of Lake Windermere.

He pressed the cloth harder onto the tray, rubbing at the tarnished corners. Years ago he'd gone to dinners, up in Knightsbridge and Mayfair. Richard Stallybrass, an art dealer, gave private gentlemen's parties, as he called them, at his flat on Belgrave Place. All very civilized. Solicitors, journalists, the odd duke or MP, there with the implicit and, in the 1970s, safe assumption that nothing would be said. Half of them had wives and children. Saul Thompson, an old friend from school, had introduced Owen to this little world and for several years Owen had been quite taken with it. He'd looked at flats in central London, encouraged by Saul to leave the suburbs and enjoy the pleasures of the city.

But there had always been Hillary and this house. She and Owen had lost their mother when they were young and it had driven them closer than many siblings were. He couldn't see himself leaving her here in Wimbledon. The idea of his sister's loneliness haunted him. One year to the next he'd put off his plans to move.

Then Saul was dead, one of the first to be claimed by the epidemic. A year later Richard Stallybrass died. Owen's connection to the gay life had always been tenuous. AIDS severed it. His work for the firm went on, work he enjoyed. And despite what an observer might assume, he hadn't been miserable. Not every fate was alike. Not everyone ended up paired off in love.

"The wine, Owen? Aren't you going to open it?"

But then he'd met Ben, and things had changed.

"Sorry?" he said.

"The wine. It's on the sideboard."

Hillary held a glass to the light, checking for smudges.

"We're certainly pulling out all the stops," he said. When she made no reply, he continued. "Believe it or not, I commented on your dress earlier but you didn't hear me. I haven't seen that one before. Have you been shopping?"

"You didn't comment on my dress, Owen. You said I was awfully dressed up."

She looked out the window over the kitchen sink. They both watched another sheet of the *Sunday Times* tumble gently into the flower beds.

"I thought we'd have our salad outside," she said. "Ben might like to see the garden."

STANDING IN STOCKINGED feet before the open door of his wardrobe, Owen pushed aside the row of gray pinstripe suits, looking for a green summer blazer he remembered wearing the year before to a garden party the firm had given out in Surrey. Brushing the dust off the shoulders, he put it on over his white shirt.

On the shelf above the suits was a boater hat—he couldn't imagine what he'd worn that to—and just behind it, barely visible, the shoe box. He paused a moment, staring at the corner of it. Ben would be here in a few hours. His first visit since he'd gone back to the States, fifteen years ago. Why now? Owen had asked himself all weekend.

"I'll be over for a conference," he'd said when Owen took the call Thursday. And yet he could so easily have come and gone from London with no word to them.

As he had each of the last three nights, Owen reached behind the boater hat and took down the shoe box. Fourteen years it had sat there untouched. Now the dust on the lid showed his fingerprints again. He listened for the sound of Hillary downstairs, then crossed the room and closed the door. Perching on the edge of the side chair, he removed the lid of the box and unfolded the last of the four letters.

November 4, 1985
Boston

Dear Hillary,

It's awkward writing when I haven't heard back from my other letters. I suppose I'll get the message soon enough. Right now I'm still bewildered. My only thought is you've decided my leaving was my own choice and not the *Globe*'s, that I have no intention of trying to get back there. I'm not sure what more I can say to convince you. I've told my editor I'll give him six months to get me reassigned to London or I'm quitting. I've been talking to people there, trying to see what might be available. It would be a lot easier if I thought this all had some purpose.

I know things got started late, that we didn't have much time before I had to leave. Owen kept you a secret for too long. But for me those were great months. I feel like a romantic clown to say I live on the memory of them, but it's not altogether untrue. I can't settle here again. I feel like I'm on a leash, everything so depressingly familiar. I'm tempted to write out all my recollections of our weekends, our evenings together, just so I can linger on them a bit more, but that would be maudlin, and you wouldn't like that—which is, of course, why I love you.

If this is over, for heaven's sake just let me know.

Yours,
Ben

Owen slid the paper back into its envelope and replaced it in the box on his lap. Dust floated in the light by the window. The rectangle of sun on the floor crept over the red pile carpet.

For most of his life he'd hated Sundays. Their gnawing stillness, the faint memories of religion. A day loneliness won. But in these last years that quiet little dread had faded. He and Hillary made a point of cooking a big breakfast and taking a walk on the common afterward. In winter they read the paper together by the fire in the front room and often walked into the town for a film in the evening. In spring and summer they spent hours in the garden. They weren't unhappy people.

From the pack on his bedside table he took a cigarette. He rolled it idly between thumb and forefinger. Would it be taken away, this life of theirs? Was Ben coming here for an answer?

He smoked the cigarette down to the filter, then returned the shoe box to its shelf and closed the door of his wardrobe. Ben was married now, had two children. That's what he'd said on the phone; they'd spoken only a minute or two. Did he still wonder why he'd never heard?

Through the window Owen could see his sister clearing their tea mugs from the garden table. There had been other men she'd gone out to dinner with over the years. A Mr. Kreske, the divorced father of a sixth-form student, who'd driven down from Putney. The maths teacher, Mr. Hamilton, had taken her to several plays in the city before returning to Scotland. Owen had tried to say encouraging things about these evenings of hers, but then the tone of her voice had always made it clear that that's all they were, evenings.

IN THE KITCHEN, Hillary stood by the sink, arranging roses in a vase.

"I see you made up the guest room," he said.

She looked directly at him, failing to register the comment. He could tell she was trying to remember something. They did that: rested their eyes on each other in moments of distraction, as you might stare at a ring on your finger.

"The guest bed. You made it up."

"Oh, yes. I did," she said, drawn back into the room. "I thought if dinner goes late and he doesn't feel like taking a train . . ."

"Of course."

Sitting again at the table, Owen picked up the tray. In it he could see his reflection, his graying hair. What would Ben look like now? he wondered.

"Chives," she said. "I forgot the chives."

They'd met through the firm, of all places. The *Globe* had Ben working on a story about differences between British and American lawyers. They went to lunch and somehow the conversation wandered. "You ask all sorts of questions," Owen could remember saying to him. And it was true. Ben had no hesitation about inquiring into Owen's private life, where he lived, how he spent his time. All in the most guileless manner, as though such questions were part of his beat.

"I hope he hasn't become allergic to anything," Hillary said, setting the chives down on the cutting board.

Though Ben had been in London nearly a year, he hadn't seen much of the place. Owen offered himself as a guide. On weekends they traveled up to Hampstead or Camden Town, or out to the East End, taking long walks, getting lunch along the way. They talked about all sorts of things. It turned out Ben too had lost a parent at a young age. When Owen heard that, he understood why he'd been drawn to Ben: he seemed to comprehend a certain register of sadness intuitively. Other than Hillary, Owen had never spoken to anyone about the death of his mother.

"I come up with lots of analogies for it," he could remember Ben saying. "Like I was burned and can't feel anything again until the flame gets that hot. Or like people's lives are over and I'm just wandering through an abandoned house. None of them really work. But you have to think the problem somehow."

Not the sort of conversation Owen had with colleagues at the office.

He picked up the cloth and wiped it again over the reflective center of the tray. Owen and his sister were so alike. Everyone said that. From the clipped tone of their voice, their gestures, right down into the byways of thought, the way they considered before speaking, said only what was needed. That she too had been attracted to Ben made perfect sense.

Hillary crossed the room and stood with her hands on

Owen's shoulders. He could feel the warmth of her palms through his cotton blazer. Unusual, this: the two of them touching.

"It'll be curious, won't it?" she said. "To see him so briefly after all this time."

"Yes."

Twenty-five years ago he and Hillary had moved into this house together. They'd thought of it as a temporary arrangement. Hillary was doing her student teaching; he'd just started with the firm and had yet to settle on a place. It seemed like the beginning of something.

"I suppose his wife couldn't come because of the children." Her thumbs rested against his collar.

She was the only person who knew of his preference for men, now that Saul and the others were gone. She'd never judged him, never raised an eyebrow.

"Interesting he should get in touch after such a gap," Owen said.

She removed her hands from his shoulders. "It strikes you as odd, does it?"

"A bit."

"I think it's thoughtful of him," she said.

"Indeed."

In the front hall, the doorbell rang.

"Goodness," Hillary said, "he's awfully early."

He listened to her footsteps as she left the room, listened as they stopped in front of the hall mirror.

"I've been with a man once myself," Ben had said on the

night Owen finally spoke to him of his feelings. Like a prayer answered, those words were. Was it such a crime he'd fallen in love?

A few more steps and then the turning of the latch.

"Oh," he heard his sister say. "Mrs. Giles. Hello."

Owen closed his eyes, relieved for the moment. Her son lived in Australia; she'd been widowed the year before. After that she'd begun stopping by on the weekends, first with the excuse of borrowing a cup of something but later just for the company.

"You're doing all right in the heat, are you?" she asked.

"Yes, we're managing," Hillary said.

Owen joined them in the hall. He could tell from the look on his sister's face she was trying to steel her courage to say they had company on the way.

"Hello there, Owen," Mrs. Giles said. "Saw your firm in the paper today."

"Did you?"

"Yes, something about the law courts. There's always news of the courts. So much of it on the telly now. Old Rumpole."

"Right," he said.

"Well . . . I was just on my way by . . . but you're occupied, I'm sure."

"No, no," Hillary said, glancing at Owen. "Someone's coming later . . . but I was just putting a kettle on."

"Really, you don't have to," Mrs. Giles said.

"Not at all."

THEY SAT IN the front room, Hillary glancing now and again at her watch. A production of *Les Misérables* had reached Perth, and Peter Giles had a leading role.

"Amazing story, don't you think?" Mrs. Giles said, sipping her tea.

The air in the room was close and Owen could feel sweat soaking the back of his shirt.

"Peter plays opposite an Australian girl. Can't quite imagine it done in that accent, but there we are. I sense he's fond of her, though he doesn't admit it in his letters."

By the portrait of their parents over the mantel, a fly buzzed. Owen sat motionless on the couch, staring over Mrs. Giles's shoulder.

His sister had always been an early riser. Up at five-thirty or six for breakfast and to prepare for class. At seven-thirty she'd leave the house in time for morning assembly. As a partner, he never had to be at the firm until well after nine. He read the *Financial Times* with his coffee and looked over whatever had come in the post. There had been no elaborate operation, no fretting over things. A circumstance had presented itself. The letters from Ben arrived. He took them up to his room. That's all there was to it.

"More tea?"

"No, thank you," Owen said.

The local council had decided on a one-way system for the town center and Mrs. Giles believed it would only make things worse. "They've done it down in Winchester. My sister says it's a terrible mess."

"Right," Owen said.

They had kissed only once, in the small hours of an August night, on the sofa in Ben's flat, light from the streetlamps coming through the high windows. Earlier, strolling back over the bridge from Battersea, Owen had told him the story of him and Hillary being sent to look for their mother: walking out across the fields to a wood where she sometimes went in the mornings; the rain starting up and soaking them before they arrived under the canopy of oaks, and looked up to see their mother's slender frame wrapped in her beige overcoat, her face lifeless, her body turning in the wind. And he'd told Ben how his sister—twelve years old—had taken him in her arms right then and there, sheltering his eyes from the awful sight, and whispered in his ear, "We will survive this, we will survive this." A story he'd never told anyone before. And when he and Ben had finished another bottle of wine, reclining there on the sofa, they'd hugged, and then they'd kissed, their hands running through each other's hair.

"I can't do this," Ben had whispered as Owen rested his head against Ben's chest.

"Smells wonderful, whatever it is you're cooking," Mrs. Giles said. Hillary nodded.

For that moment before Ben had spoken, as he lay in his arms, Owen had believed in the fantasy of love as the creator, your life clay in its hands.

"I should check the food. Owen, why don't you show Mrs. Giles a bit of the garden. She hasn't seen the delphiniums, I'm sure."

"Of course," he said, looking into his sister's taut smile.

"I suspect I've mistreated my garden," Mrs. Giles said as the two of them reached the bottom of the lawn. "John it was who had the green thumb. I'm just a bungler really."

The skin of her hands was mottled and soft looking. The gold ring she still wore hung rather loosely on her finger.

"I think Ben and I might have a weekend away," Hillary had said one evening in the front room as they watched the evening news. The two of them had only met a few weeks before. An accident really, Hillary in the city on an errand, coming to drop something by for Owen, deciding at the last minute to join them for dinner. When the office phoned the restaurant in the middle of the meal, Owen had to leave the two of them alone.

A weekend at the cottage on Lake Windermere is what they had.

Owen had always thought of himself as a rational person, capable of perspective. As a school boy, he'd read *Othello. O, beware, my lord, of jealousy! It is the green-eyed monster, which doth mock the meat it feeds on.* What paltry aid literature turned out to be when the feelings were yours and not others'.

"Funny, I miss him in the most peculiar ways," Mrs. Giles said. "We'd always kept the chutney over the stove, and as we only ever had it in the evenings, he'd be there to fetch it. Ridiculous to use a stepladder for the chutney, if you think about it. Does just as well on the counter."

"Yes," Owen said.

They stared together into the blue flowers.

"I expect it won't be long before I join him," she said.

"No, you're in fine shape, surely."

"Doesn't upset me—the idea. It used to, but not anymore. I've been very lucky. He was a good person."

Owen could hear the telephone ringing in the house.

"Could you get that?" Hillary called from the kitchen.

"I apologize, I—"

"No, please, carry on," Mrs. Giles said.

He left her there and passing through the dining room, crossed the hall to the phone.

"Owen, it's Ben Hansen."

"Ben."

"Look, I feel terrible about this, but I'm not going to be able to make it out there tonight."

"Oh."

"Yeah, the meetings are running late here and I'm supposed to give this talk, it's all been pushed back. Horrible timing, I'm afraid."

Owen could hear his sister closing the oven door, the water coming on in the sink.

"I'm sorry about that. It's a great pity. I know Hillary was looking forward to seeing you. We both were."

"I was looking forward to it myself, I really was," he said. "Have you been well?"

Owen laughed. "Me? Yes. I've been fine. Everything's very much the same on this end . . . It does seem awfully long ago you were here."

For a moment, neither of them spoke.

Standing there in the hall, Owen felt a sudden longing. He imagined Ben as he often saw him in his mind's eye, tall and thin, half a step ahead on the Battersea Bridge, hands scrunched into his pockets. And he pictured the men he sometimes saw holding hands in Soho or Piccadilly. In June, perhaps on this very Sunday, thousands marched. He wanted to tell Ben what it felt like to pass two men on the street like that, how he had always in a sense been afraid.

"You're still with the firm?"

"Yes," Owen said. "That's right." And he wanted to say how frightened he'd been watching his friend Saul's ravaged body die, how the specter of disease had made him timid. How he, Ben, had seemed a refuge.

"And with you, things have been well?"

He listened as Ben described his life—columnist now for the paper, the children beginning school; he heard the easy, slightly weary tone in his voice—a parent's fatigue. And he wondered how Ben remembered them. Were Hillary and Owen Simpson just two people he'd met on a year abroad ages ago? Had he been coming here for answers, or did he just have a free evening and a curiosity about what had become of them?

What did it matter now? There would be no revelation tonight. He was safe again.

"Might you be back over at some point?" he asked. He sensed their conversation about to end and felt on the edge of panic.

"Definitely. It's one of the things I wanted to ask you about. Judy and I were thinking of bringing the kids—maybe next summer—and I remembered you rented that place up north. Is there a person to call about getting one of those?"

"The cottages? . . . Yes, of course."

"Yeah, that would be great. I'll try to give you a call when we're ready to firm up some plans."

"And Judy? She's well?"

"Sure, she's heard all about you, wants to meet you both sometime."

"That would be terrific," Owen said, the longing there again.

"Ben?"

"Yes?"

"Who is it?" Hillary asked, stepping into the hall, drying her hands with a dishcloth. A red amulet their mother had worn hung round her neck, resting against the front of her linen dress.

"Ben," he mouthed.

Her face stiffened slightly.

"Hillary's just here," he said into the phone. "Why don't you have a word?" He held the receiver out to her.

"He can't make it."

"Is that right?" she said, staring straight through him. She took the phone. Owen walked back into the dining room; by the sideboard, he paused.

"No, no, don't be silly," he heard his sister say. "It's quite all right."

"A BEAUTIFUL EVENING, isn't it?" Mrs. Giles said as he stepped back onto the terrace. The air was mild now, the sun beginning to shade into the trees. Clouds like distant mountains had appeared on the horizon.

"Yes," he said, imagining the evening view of the lake from the garden of their cottage, the way they checked the progress of the days by which dip in the hills the sun disappeared behind.

Mrs. Giles stood from the bench. "I should be getting along."

He walked her down the side of the house and out the gate. Though the sky was still bright, the streetlamps had begun to flicker on. Farther up the street a neighbor watered her lawn.

"Thank you for the tea."

"Not at all," he said.

"It wasn't bad news just now, I hope."

"No, no," he said. "Just a friend calling."

"That's good, then." She hesitated by the low brick wall that separated their front gardens. "Owen, there was just one thing I wanted to mention. In my sitting room, the desk over in the corner, in the top drawer there. I've put a letter in. You understand. I wanted to make sure someone would know where to look. Nothing to worry about, of course, nothing dramatic . . . but in the event . . . you see?"

He nodded, and she smiled back at him, her eyes beginning to water. Owen watched her small figure as she turned and passed through her gate, up the steps, and into her house.

He stayed awhile on the sidewalk, gazing onto the common: the expanse of lawn, white goalposts on the football pitch set against the trees. A long shadow, cast by their house and the others along this bit of street, fell over the playing field. He watched it stretching slowly to the chestnut trees, the darkness slowly climbing their trunks, beginning to shade the leaves of the lower branches.

In the house, he found Hillary at the kitchen table, hands folded in her lap. She sat perfectly still, staring into the garden. For a few minutes they remained like that, Owen at the counter, neither of them saying a word. Then his sister got up and passing him as though he weren't there, opened the oven door.

"Right," she said. "It's done."

They ate in the dining room, in the fading light, with the silver and the crystal. Roses, pink and white, stood in a vase at the center of the table. As the plates were already out, Hillary served her chicken marsala on their mother's china. The candles remained unlit in the silver candlesticks.

"He'll be over again," Owen said. Hillary nodded. They finished their dinner in silence. Afterward, neither had the appetite for the strawberries set out on the polished tray.

"I'll do these," he said when they'd stacked the dishes on the counter. He squeezed the green liquid detergent into the baking dish and watched it fill with water. "I could pour you a brandy if you like," he said over his shoulder. But when he turned he saw his sister had left the room.

He rinsed the bowls and plates and arranged them neatly in the rows of the dishwasher. Under the warm running water, he sponged the wineglasses clean and set them to dry on the rack. When he'd finished, he turned the taps off, and then the kitchen was quiet.

He poured himself a scotch and took a seat at the table. The door to the garden had been left open and in the shadows he could make out the azalea bush and the cluster of rhododendron. Up the lane from where they'd lived as children, there was a manor with elaborate gardens and a moat around the house. An old woman they called Mrs. Montague lived there and she let them play on the rolling lawns and in the labyrinth of the topiary hedge. They would play for hours in the summer, chasing each other along the embankments, pretending to fish in the moat with a stick and string. He won their games of hide-and-go-seek because he never closed his eyes completely, and could see which way she ran. He could still remember the peculiar anger and frustration he used to feel after he followed her to her hiding place and tapped her on the head. He imagined that garden now, the blossoms of its flowers drinking in the cooler night air, the branches of its trees rejuvenating in the darkness.

From the front room, he heard a small sound—a moan let out in little breaths—and realized it was the sound of his sister crying.

He had ruined her life. He knew that now in a way he'd always tried not to know it—with certainty. For years he'd allowed himself to imagine she had forgotten Ben, or at least stopped remembering. He stood up from the table and crossed the room but stopped at the entrance to the hall. What consolation could he give her now?

Standing there, listening to her tears, he remembered the last time he'd heard them, so long ago it seemed like the memory of a former life: a summer morning when she'd returned from university, and they'd walked together over the fields in a brilliant sunshine and come to the oak trees, their green leaves shining, their branches heavy with acorns. She'd wept then for the first time in all the years since their mother had taken herself away. And Owen had been there to comfort her—his turn at last, after all she had done to protect him.

At the sound of his footsteps entering the hall, Hillary went quiet. He stopped again by the door to the front room. Sitting at the breakfast table, reading those letters from America, it wasn't only Ben's affection he'd envied. Being replaced. That was the fear. The one he'd been too weak to master.

Holding on to the banister, he slowly climbed the stairs, his feet pressing against the worn patches of the carpet. They might live in this silence the rest of their lives, he thought.

In his room, he walked to the window and looked again over the common.

When they were little they'd gone to the village on Sundays to hear the minister talk. Of charity and sacrifice. A Norman church with hollows worked into the stones of the floor by centuries of parishioners. He could still hear the congregation singing, *Bring me my bow of burning gold! Bring me my arrows of desire!* Their mother had sung with them. Plaintive voices rising. *And did those feet in ancient time walk upon England's mountains green?* Owen could remember wanting to believe something about it all, if not the words of the Book perhaps the sorrow he heard in the music, the longing of people's song. He hadn't been in a church since his mother's funeral. Over the years, views from the train or the sight of this common in evening had become his religion, absorbing the impulse to imagine larger things.

Looking over it now, he wondered at the neutrality of the grass and the trees and the houses beyond, how in their stillness they neither judged nor forgave. He stared across the playing field a moment longer. And then, calmly, he crossed to the wardrobe and took down the box.

SITTING IN THE front room, Hillary heard her brother's footsteps overhead and then the sound of his door closing. Her tears had dried and she felt a stony kind of calm, gazing into the wing chair opposite—an old piece of their parents' furniture. Threads showed at the armrests, and along the front edge the ticking had come loose. At first they'd meant to get rid of so many things, the faded rugs, the heavy felt curtains, but their parents' possessions had settled in the house, and then there seemed no point.

In the supermarket checkout line, she sometimes glanced at the cover of a decor magazine, a sunny room with blond wood floors, bright solid colors, a white sheet on a white bed. The longing for it usually lasted only a moment. She knew she'd be a foreigner in such a room.

She sipped the last of her wine and put the glass down on the coffee table. Darkness had fallen now and in the window she saw the reflection of the lamp and the mantel and the bookcase.

"Funny, isn't it? How it happens." That's all her friend Miriam Franks would ever say if the conversation turned onto the topic of why neither of them had married. Hillary would nod and recall one of the evenings she'd spent with Ben up at the cottage, sitting in the garden, talking of Owen, thinking to herself she could only ever be with someone who understood her brother as well as Ben did.

She switched off the light in the front room and walked to the kitchen. Owen had wiped down the counters, set everything back in its place. For a moment, she thought she might cry again. Her brother had led such a cramped life, losing his friends, scared of what people might know. She'd loved him so fiercely all these years, the fears and hindrances had felt like her own. What good, then, had her love been? she wondered as she pulled the French doors shut.

Upstairs, Owen's light was still on, but she didn't knock or say good night as she usually did. Across the hall in her own room, she closed the door behind her. The little stack of letters lay on her bed. Years ago she had read them, after rummaging for a box at Christmastime. Ben was married by then, as she'd found out when she called. Her anger had lasted a season or two but she had held her tongue, remembering the chances Owen had to leave her and how he never had.

Standing over the bed now, looking down at the pale blue envelopes, she was glad her brother had let go of them at last. Tomorrow they would have supper in the kitchen. He would offer to leave this house, and she would tell him that was the last thing she wanted.

Putting the letters aside, she undressed. When she'd climbed into bed, she reached up and turned the switch of her bedside lamp. For an instant, lying in the sudden darkness, she felt herself there again in the woods, covering her brother's eyes as she gazed up into the giant oak.

WAR'S END

HE HAS SEEN these cliffs before, in picture books. He has seen the wide beaches and the ruined cathedral. Ellen, his wife, she has shown him. In the taxi from the station, Paul looks over the golf course, and there is Saint Andrews: the bell tower, rows of huddled stone houses, the town set out on a promontory, out over the blue-black sea. Farther, in the distance, a low bank of rain cloud stretches over the water;

waves emerge from the mist. He follows them into shore, watching them swell and crest, churning against the rocks.

Ellen reaches across the back seat and takes his hand.

They have come here for her to use a library at the university. They have paid for their trip with the last of her grant money and a credit card. Paul's latest psychiatrist, the one they can't really afford, has said a change of scenery might help, a break in the routine of empty days. He's been gone from work a year now, low as he's ever been and tired. In their apartment, in a college town in Pennsylvania, he has lain in bed in the early morning hours as Ellen slept beside him, and known that her life would be easier if he were gone. He's been too fatigued to plan.

Until now.

Staring at the dark face of the cliffs, his mind quickens enough to see how it might happen, and for a moment, sitting there in the taxi, holding his wife's hand, he feels relief.

AFTER CHECKING INTO the hotel and unpacking their things, they go looking for a restaurant. The main street is cobbled, lined with two-story stone buildings, dirty beige or gray. A drizzle has begun to fall, dotting the plate glass windows of the shops closed for the night. The pubs have stopped serving food. They wander further and come to a restaurant on the town square, a mock American diner lit with traffic signals, the walls hung with road signs for San Diego and Gary, Indiana.

"Charming," Ellen says, opening the front door.

Paul hangs back, stilled by a dread of the immediate future, the dispiriting imitations he sees through the windows, a fear of what it will feel like to be in there, a sense that commitment to it could be a mistake, that perhaps they should keep going. Though he doesn't want that either, having already sensed an abandoned quality to this town: the students gone for their Easter break, the pubs nearly empty, the dirty right angle where the sidewalk meets the foundation stones of a darkened bank, the crumpled flyer that lies there, all of it gaining on him now, this scene, these objects, their malignancy. He tries to recall the relief of just an hour ago: that soon this will end, the accusatory glare of the inanimate world. But there on the pavement in halogen streetlight is a scattering of sand that appears to him as if in the tight focus of a camera's lens, sharper than his eyes can bear.

He takes a steadying breath, as the doctor told him to when the world of objects becomes so lucid he feels he is being crushed by their presence.

"You sure about this?" he asks.

"It's late—we might as well," Ellen says. "We can find something better tomorrow."

He could stop her, try to explain, but as she looks back at him from the doorway he can see her nascent concern in the slight tilt of her head. She will be looking for signs of improvement in him, indications the trip was a good idea. He will want time alone in the days ahead. If she worries too much now, she may hesitate to go by herself to the library. It's the first time in months he's been capable of an instrumental thought, a weighing of needs.

"All right," he says, and follows her through the door.

At their table, the coffee stains and salt crystals on the red-and-white checkered oilcloth press him back in his chair; escaping them, he looks across the room to see a broad-faced old woman, her skin the color of a whitish moon. She sits at a table by the kitchen sipping a mug of tea. Their eyes meet for a moment, neither of them looking away. They stare straight at each other, expressionless, oddly intimate, like spies acknowledging each other's presence in a room of strangers. She nods, smiles weakly, turns away.

When the waitress arrives, Ellen orders her food. Then there is silence. Paul reads the description of the chicken sandwich again. From the speakers, he hears the smooth, crooning voices of the Doobie Brothers.

Time barely moves.

"Paul, you know what you want?"

He looks into Ellen's face, the slight rise of her eyebrow, a sign of apprehension, so familiar from the days she first saw him depressed, a year before they married, when for no apparent reason his basic faith in the world, the faith that there is a purpose in working or eating, dissolved, and she came to his apartment day after day with her books, conversation, news—patient and loving. Many times he's wondered why, after seeing him that way, she still married him. She was wrong to do it, he knows now, seeing her strained eyes and pursed lips, the way the old sympathy must fight against frustration. He is the chain and the weight. No matter how she struggles, he will pull her under eventually. Getting out of the house, out of the solipsism of blank days, coming to this foreign place, he can see it all more clearly.

The waitress stares.

"Honey? What are you going to have?" Ellen asks, trying after a long day's journey not to sound impatient.

Silence stretches on.

"He'll have a chicken sandwich," Ellen says at last.

IN THE BATHROOM at the hotel, he stands before the mirror trying to recall his reason for being there. Electric light shines evenly on the sink's white porcelain. Cool air slides from the windowsill across the floor onto his bare feet. Water swells on the lip of the faucet.

From the bedroom he hears Ellen's voice. She seems to be talking about a friend of hers, a woman at the college who like Ellen has no permanent position, and was apparently just let go. There is something about courses not filled. She asks a question he doesn't follow. He tries to piece together what he's heard but it's no good.

"You all right in there?"

He opens his fist and sees the pill he is supposed to take flaking in the sweat of his palm.

Ten times, maybe even twenty, he has sat on a doctor's couch and answered the same battery of questions about his sleep and interest in sex, his appetite and sense of despair; and he's said, yes, there was an uncle and a grandmother who, looking back, seemed unhappy in more than the usual ways;

and yes, there were his parents, who divorced, his mother who always had a few drinks after dinner; and no, he doesn't hear voices or believe there is a plot to undo him. At the end of each of the hours, he's listened to the doctor's brief talk about the new combination they'd like to try, how at first it might make him nauseous or tired or anxious. For years he's done as he was told, and for stretches of time he's felt like a living person. Then the undertow returns. Ellen hears of a better doctor. Again he must answer the questions. He's always doubted the purpose of the drugs. Despite all the explanations, he's never been able to rid himself of the conviction that his experience has a meaning. That the crushing pulse of specificity he so often sees teeming in the physical world is no distortion. That it is there to be seen if one has the eyes. He's been told this is a romantic notion, a dangerous thing to cling to, bad advice for the mentally ill. Perhaps it is. Though the opposite has always seemed more frightening to him, lonelier—the idea that so much of him was a pure and blinded waste.

"I'm fine," he says softly, rinsing the damp powder into the drain.

In bed, Ellen leans her head on his chest, laying a hand flat on his stomach. There is nothing sexual about her touch. There has been none of that for a long time. She is thirty-four and would like to have a child. He begins, as he has so often, to think of all the things he does not provide her, but knowing the list is endless, he stops.

"You feel nice and warm," she says.

He runs his hand through her hair. She has never worn

perfume or makeup, which for him has always added to her beauty, the lack of facade.

"You all set for the library tomorrow?"

"Yeah," she says, nodding her head against his chest.

She's come to read correspondence from the Second World War, part of her research on the lives of women on the home front. Her real interests are in the political history of the time, but her adviser has told her there is a glut of scholarship on the topic and it isn't the best idea if she wants to find a faculty position. She's thought about ignoring his advice, but when Paul stopped working, she decided it was best to be practical.

He remembers their meeting for the first time, at a friend's house, where they sat in a bay window overlooking a garden. No matter what she spoke of, she seemed so optimistic: her work, their friends at the party, the cut of his jacket—it was all good. Those first months he would come to her apartment in the afternoons when he'd finished his teaching at the high school. He'd do his correcting at the kitchen table while she worked at her desk in the bedroom. It was as if he'd been invited into a parallel world, a place where small pleasures—like knowing she was in the other room—could be a daily thing. She had a bemused look on her face when one evening he tried to explain he wasn't feeling well. They were sitting on the porch of her apartment after supper, a pop song, as he remembers it, coming from the window of her downstairs neighbor.

"You're too hard on yourself," she said. "That school

wears you out. You need more sleep." Her voice had a kindly tone. If he hadn't known before, he knew then she'd never experienced the kind of dread he was trying to describe. It didn't matter, he told himself then. That she loved him, that was enough. It wasn't realistic to expect acknowledgment would ever be complete.

"I'll just get started at the library tomorrow, just a few hours in the morning," she says, reaching up to kiss him good night. "Then we can take a walk around, see the beach."

He touches his hand to her face.

"All right," he says, switching off the bedside lamp.

EARLY MORNING, A pewter gray light hangs in the middle of the room, leaving the corners obscured, blurring the outlines of the sitting chair and bureau.

He dresses quietly; quietly he closes the door behind him. The air outside is cold, mist blanketing the streets. He makes his way up toward the castle, and from there onto the path leading alongside the wall of the cathedral grounds. Opposite is the cliff, grass running to its edge. He walks to the verge. He can hear the slosh and fizz of the sea below, the deep knock of a boulder being rocked in place by the waves. All of it invisible down there in the fog.

It is better this way, he thinks.

" 'Scuse me, dear, could you give me a hand?" a voice behind him says.

He turns to see an old woman buttoned in a green wool coat. She stands no more than a yard away, holding a grocery bag. He can't understand how she's come this near without his notice. As he looks more closely, he sees it is the old woman from the restaurant, her brown eyes set in wrinkled skin.

"Didn't mean to scare you, dear. Just that I've dropped a bit of the shopping. Shouldn't have brought Polly down before stopping at the house." She glances back along the cliff, where a white terrier emerges from the mist. A brown paper bag lies on the ground before her.

Mutely, he kneels to retrieve it.

"The chemist—always a new something or other," she mutters. When she has the bag safely in hand, she says, "You're American."

Paul stares at her, as if at an apparition.

"Come for the course, have you? . . . Have you come over for the golf?"

He shakes his head.

"Air force? Over at Leuchars, are you?"

"No. My wife. She's . . ."

"She's what, dear? . . . At the university?"

He nods.

"Right. Lots of the foreigners over for that. Nothing like the golf, though. Last summer was dreadful. We had the British Open. You'd think Christ had risen on the eighteenth green. More telly people than putters as far as I could tell. Awful. You live in Texas?"

He shakes his head. "Pennsylvania."

"Is that near Texas?"

"No."

She leans down to pat the head of her terrier, who has scurried up to meet them. "Your wife's in the books and you've got the day to yourself."

Paul says nothing. She comes a step closer, barely two feet from him. "Not an easy place to entertain yourself," she says, leaning her head forward. "Without the golf, I mean." She searches his face, as though straining to read the fine print of a map. "Would you like to come for a cup of tea?"

HE DOES NOT know why he goes with her. She is here and has asked and so he goes.

They walk down past the clock tower. She moves slowly, stopping to look back for the dog, checking her bags and packages. She speaks of the university students, complains of the noise they make during term, says the tourists are generally polite but she doesn't like all the coach buses.

They take a right turn, then a left down a narrow street of two-story houses. At the door of one, the old woman pauses and finding the key in the pocket of her coat, inserts it in the lock. The dog runs ahead into the darkened hall and the old woman follows, leaving Paul standing at the entrance.

As he steps into the house, a heavy, warm odor envelops him. His first reaction is to close his nostrils, breathe only through his mouth. Then, tentatively, he sniffs. It is flesh he smells, not sweat or the dankness of a locker room, but something close. A rotting.

Breathing through his mouth, he advances down the hall toward a light that has come on in the next room. He won't want to stay long, he thinks, wondering how anyone could live with such a smell. She'll comment on it, make an apology of some sort, he feels sure. But when he reaches the kitchen, she is calmly stowing her groceries.

"Have a seat, dear. Tea won't be a moment."

Though it is day, the curtains are drawn and a naked bulb provides the only light. He perches on the edge of a chair by the kitchen table, sampling the air again. The stench tickles his nostrils.

The kitchen looks a bit disheveled, the counters cluttered with jars and mugs, but otherwise it is like any other kitchen. There is nothing here to explain such an odor. He imagines naked, sweating bodies packed into the other rooms of the house.

"I've got some biscuits round here somewhere, what did I do with them? Do you take milk and sugar?"

Watching the old woman shuffle past the sink, he feels disoriented and tries to confirm to himself where he is, the day of the week, the country they are in.

"Milk, dear?"

"I saw you in the restaurant last night, didn't I?" he says.

"Yes, dear, you did. Sometimes I come and sit in the evenings, if I can find someone for Albert. He's my grandson. You'll meet him."

She arranges cookies on a plate. "Have you been visiting elsewhere, then?"

"We passed through Edinburgh," he says.

"Terrible place. Full of strangers. What do you do in the States?"

Paul has to repeat her words to himself before replying.

"I used to teach," he says.

For a moment, he sees the classroom on the third floor of the high school, its scratched plastic windows, chairs of chrome metal, beige desks affixed, a map of America, the portrait of Lincoln tacked to the back wall. The students staring, waiting for him to speak.

"How wonderful. Noble profession, teaching is," she says, placing a mug on the table beside him. "There's sugar there if you like."

She puts her own mug down and takes a seat opposite.

"And what is it you taught?"

"History," he says.

"Dates. Yes. Albert's very good with dates . . . Are you a father?"

"No," he says, wondering why he is here.

"A mixed blessing children are, of course. Up to all sorts of things. When they're young, though—nothing like it. You taught young ones, did you?"

"Teenagers."

"Difficult they are."

There is a pause. The old woman leans forward in her chair. "You're tired," she says.

"Sorry?"

"You're tired, dear, under the eyes. You've been sleeping poorly."

Paul feels a surge of anger. He wants to yell at the old woman. How dare she presume? But there is something so frank in her expression, so lacking in judgment, he can't bring himself to do it.

"Jet lag, I suppose," he says.

He sips at his mug. The odor leaks in. He feels he might heave the liquid up.

"Have you ever had fresh mutton?" she asks.

He shakes his head.

"An excellent meat. My friend Sibyl gets it straight from the abattoir. Rosemary, wee spot of mint jelly. Quite delicious. Perhaps you might come for dinner. I doubt they'll be giving you any Scottish meat in the hotels."

The smell has got to him now and he is beginning to feel dizzy. "What time is it?"

"It's early, dear. Just gone half eight."

"I should go back."

"There's no hurry, surely." She stirs her tea. "Just out for a walk this morning, were you?"

He looks up at her. "My wife," he says. "She'll be waking up. I really have to go." He stands up from his chair.

"Well, if you must rush, then—pity though, you've just arrived. But there we are, you'll come tomorrow. For dinner—two o'clock. It'll rain in the morning."

"No . . . I don't know."

"Not to worry about it now," she says, patting him on the shoulder. They move into the front hall. "It's getting cold this time of year. The haar will cover the town by the end of the week. You'll want to keep inside for that."

She holds open the front door. When he steps onto the

street, he breathes in the cold air, finding it less of a relief than he'd hoped.

HE WALKS TO the end of the cobbled street, looking one way and the other, forgetting the route that brought him here. Steps lead to doors on the second floor of row houses, smoke rising from squat chimneys. A child passes on a bicycle. He watches the little figure vanish around a corner and begins moving in the same direction.

He follows the sound of voices down onto Market Street. In the square, vendors arrange stalls of plants and second-hand books. A man wearing a placard reads from the book of Revelation, while his wife, standing silently by, passes literature to those who will take it. There are etchings of the seashore in the dry basin of the fountain. He walks slowly through, past tables covered with baked goods and china, testing the scent of the air as he goes.

"Where have you been?" Ellen cries as he enters the lobby. "Where in the world have you been?"

He looks at her with what he imagines is a pleading expression.

"Paul," she says, her voice quavering. She puts her arms around him, holds his head against her shoulder.

"Why didn't you wake me? What's going on?"

He's used all the words he has to describe his state to her. He could only repeat them now. A selfish repetition. How many times will he ask for a reassurance he will never believe?

This should have ended by now.

He holds on to her, grabbing her more tightly because he can think of nothing to say.

THEY SPEND THE rest of that morning in the room. Paul sits in a chair by the window, while Ellen reads the paper. She has called the library to let the curator know she will be starting a day later.

Her way of coping with him has changed over the years. She's read books and articles about depression and its symptoms, spoken to the psychiatrists he sees, tackled the problem like the researcher she is. She knows the clinical details, reminding him always it is a chemical problem, a treatable disease: eventually a doctor will find the right formula.

From the window, he sees a man across the street depositing a letter in a mailbox and he wonders what the inside of the man's leather glove would smell of. He runs a hand under his nose, sniffing his palm.

"Do you want to call Dr. Gormley?" Ellen asks.

His glance drops, freezing on the wool ticking of the armchair; strands of dust settle on the blue fibers. He shakes his head.

THAT NIGHT, WHEN he cannot sleep he goes into the bathroom and pees. He splashes urine on the edge of the bowl, then gets on his hands and knees to sniff the rim. He smells the cracks in the tile, the damp bath mat, his wife's underwear, the hair and skin in the drain of the tub. He runs his finger along the back of the medicine cabinet's shelf and tastes the gray-white dust. None of it comes close to the stench in that house.

ALL THE NEXT morning it rains, as the old woman said it would. They eat lunch in the nearly empty dining room of the hotel. Across the way, a German couple argues quietly over a map. Ellen suggests that Paul come back to the library with her, he could read the British papers there. She only needs a day or two, she says, then they can take the train back to Edinburgh, see more of the city.

There is a fragment of tea leaf on the rim of her cup; a sheen to the softening butter; a black fly brushing its feelers on the white cloth of the table. He pictures the library and at once fears some constriction he imagines he will experience there. It is the familiar fear of being anywhere at all, of committing to the decision to stay in one place.

"I think I'll take a walk," he says.

"Did you take the pill this morning?" she asks. There is no impatience in her voice. She has trained herself over the years to control that, which only reminds him of how he's weighed on her, whittled her down to this cautious caring. He nods, though once again he's disposed of the tablet in the bathroom, knowing she will count them.

After she leaves for the library, Paul sets out across the square, past the tables of books and china, heading into the narrow lanes. As he comes to the house and reaches out to knock on the low door, it opens and the old woman steps aside to let him enter.

"Good afternoon," she says. "We never made our introductions yesterday. I'm Mrs. McLaggan."

"Paul Lewis," he says.

"Right. Mr. Lewis. I'm glad you've come." They walk down the hall into the kitchen. "I'll just be a minute," she says, heading into the other room. It's then he sniffs the air, finding it as thick and rank as the day before. A light comes on in the next room, the old woman calls to him, and Paul walks through the doorway.

Running along the far side of the room, completely obscuring the windows, is a wall of clear plastic gallon buckets filled with what appears to be petroleum jelly. They've been arranged in a single row and stacked from floor to ceiling. Along the adjacent wall stands a metal clothes rack on wheels holding twenty or more identical blue track suits. A sideboard across from this is laid with dishes of lamb, potatoes, and string beans. Mrs. McLaggan stands in the middle of the room under another naked lightbulb. At the center is a table set for two.

The low ceiling, the electric light, the pale brown walls, the strange provisions all give the room the feel of a way station on some forgotten trade route, or a bunker yet to hear news of the war's end.

"Now, dear, I hope you'll just help yourself to everything," Mrs. McLaggan says, standing by her chair.

He is not hungry but fills a plate anyway and sits.

"Mrs. Lewis is getting on well at the university, then, is she?" she says, once she's served herself and taken a seat.

"Yes."

For a minute or two, they eat in silence.

"I was thinking perhaps you might meet Albert today," she says. "I've told him about you. Difficult to know sometimes, but I think he's keen to see you."

"Do you do this often?"

"What's that, dear?"

"Having guests you don't know—strangers."

Mrs. McLaggan looks down at her plate and smiles. "You're not a stranger here," she says. "In the restaurant the other night . . . How should I say it? . . . I recognized you somehow, not like I'd met you or such, but nonetheless. And then yesterday morning . . ." Her voice trails off.

"Would you like a glass of wine?" she asks. For years he's had no alcohol because of medication—the warnings and the caveats.

"Sure," he says.

She pours them each a glass. "My grandson's not well, you see." After saying this, she pauses, her eyes wandering left, then right, as if deciding how to proceed.

"Glenda, my daughter—she was awfully young when she had him. Father was some fellow I never saw. Course the old codgers round here never tire of saying, 'Wasn't so back in our day, was it then?' I don't know, though. Seems to me the world's always had plenty of trouble to spare a bit for the girls . . . I suppose what's different is she went off, left Albert with me. Would've been harder when I was young, that would—a woman going out into the world like that. But there we are. Manchester she went to first. Then London for a spell."

She sips her wine.

"You try not to judge . . . Course when Albert got sick I rang. To tell her he'd gone into hospital. Tried the last number I had for her. No answer though, line disconnected. Been three years he's been ill now."

She looks up at Paul and smiles, wanly. "Here I am nattering on about my troubles."

"It's all right," he says. He's finished half a glass of wine. With the scent of it, the smell of the house has risen into his head again, but he fights it less now.

"You seem like a very sympathetic man," she says.

When the meal is finished, they return to the kitchen and Mrs. McLaggan puts a kettle on the stove. "Shall we go up, then, and see Albert?"

"All right."

She makes the tea and sets it out on a tray. Paul follows her up the stairs. They pass along a narrow hallway. The smell is stronger here. They stop at a door and she gestures for him to open it.

"It's difficult at first," she says.

The air in the room is so heavy with stench he feels like he's being pressed to a man's body and made to breathe through the filter of his skin—a familiar scent raised to a sickening power. It's a small space with one eaved window, open at the top. In the corner, a boy of ten or twelve lies on a bed. He wears a blue track suit marked with greasy spots. His face and neck are red and crusted with dry skin. Wet sores and patches of rawness cover his wrists and the backs of his hands. He barely moves as they enter, shifting his head only slightly.

"Albert, this is Mr. Lewis. The man I told you about. He's come for a visit."

Mrs. McLaggan sets the tray down on the bedside table. The boy looks at Paul, his eyes caught in folds of livid pink and red.

"Have the armchair, there, why don't you?" the old woman says. She perches on a low stool pulled up next to the bed and pours a cup of tea. She holds it in one hand, a spoon in the other, lowering the liquid to the boy's swollen mouth.

"It's chamomile," she says softly. "You like chamomile."

The boy strains to raise his head from the pillow; his lips tremble as he sips.

" 'Scuse him, Mr. Lewis, if he doesn't say much. The pain's been bad lately, hasn't it, Albert?" She turns to Paul. "I swear Job never suffered like this."

At the end of the bed, he can see the boy's feet, where brownish white calluses thick as hide cover his soles.

"Remember, Albert? I told you Mr. Lewis is a history man. I'm sure he knows all about all sorts of things."

When she has finished with the tea, she puts it aside and unzips the boy's top. His chest is covered in the same red mix of sores and flaking skin. Taking up a cloth, she dips it in a bucket by the stool and begins to gently lather ointment onto Albert's stomach. He sighs as the jelly is spread over him.

"Henry the Second is Albert's favorite. We've just started reading about him, haven't we? Do you know anything about Henry the Second, Mr. Lewis?"

The stench and the sight of the boy is nearly overwhelming Paul and he feels he might faint.

"I . . . I haven't read about all that . . . not since college," he manages after a pause. "It was American history I did."

"But you remember some of the medieval bits, no?" she says, hopefully.

Breathing through his mouth, he manages to calm the swoon in his stomach. The boy stares at him with a longing that seems to Paul neither desperate nor afraid. It is just a longing, a want.

"He was a remarkable king," Paul says, transfixed by the boy's gaze. "I remember that much."

"There, you see. He knows all about him. I'll wager he's got stories you've not heard yet. Perhaps he'll tell you one. Would you tell Albert a story?"

Paul nods, having no idea what he will say.

"Has your grandmother told you about Stephen?" he asks, recalling the name from some course taken years before.

Albert manages a small shake of the head.

"Well . . . that's the king that preceded Henry, and he was the son of . . ." His mind goes blank. Mrs. McLaggan raises the cloth onto the boy's chest. Paul sees the little white pustules dotting the red skin; the tarnished gold ring on the old woman's finger; beyond the bed, cartoon figures on the faded wallpaper.

"I don't remember who he was the son of, but in any case, they made a deal . . . Stephen could rule if his line stopped with him, and Henry would come to the throne . . ."

Again Paul fumbles, recalling the giant lecture hall where a man with a German accent had taught early Europe.

"It wasn't long before Stephen died. And Henry was king, at eighteen or twenty, I think, monarch of the largest empire in Europe."

When his voice ceases, it seems quieter in the room than when he began, the boy's eyes calmer.

"He married," Paul says. And again a memory he didn't know he had arrives.

"Eleanor of Aquitaine. She was the daughter of a man who ruled part of France, and by marrying her Henry added the land to his domain. They had many children. The sons fought with their father, though, terribly. And Eleanor, she sided against Henry as well . . ."

He tells the boy of Eleanor's first imprisonment in Normandy, describing the cell, embellishing, and the story of how Henry kept her for years at Winchester and Salisbury. As he speaks, the old woman draws the cloth across Albert's forehead. Paul remembers Thomas à Becket, slain at Canterbury, the knights acting on Henry's angry words, which Paul repeats now, as his teacher repeated them to him: *"'Will no one rid me of this troublesome priest?'* And so they returned to England and stabbed him, inside his own cathedral. Henry's friend since childhood, his conscience."

Stringing the memories together now, he begins to paint the picture of the restless king who for thirty-five years never slept in one bed more than a fortnight, ranging over his vast possessions, battling thankless sons. There are the struggles with the barons, the war over France, the last imprisonment of Eleanor. Soon the tale flows easily, of channel crossings and broken treaties, and he opens the Plantagenet world up like a flower for the boy, knowing the hunger for the dramatic statement, the declarations of war, castle sieges, men fighting to the death, victors standing on the ramparts, broadswords held over their heads—all the beautiful wealth and violence of a boy's imagination.

"Better than any book, that was," Mrs. McLaggan says when he is finished. She folds the cloth and places it in the wastebasket. "Your granny can't do that, Albert, can she?"

There is just the hint of a nod from Albert.

"I'm sure I've confused some of it," he says. "There's a lot to tell—Richard, and the Crusades."

The light in the room has begun to fade. Ellen will have left the library now, he thinks. She will have walked to the hotel and found him not there. It seems so unlikely that they are still in the same town, that he has not traveled farther than that.

"We're going to let you rest now," the old woman says. "Perhaps Mr. Lewis will come back tomorrow. Would you like that?" She leans down and touches her lips to the boy's cheek.

DOWNSTAIRS IN THE hall, as she is walking Paul to the door, Mrs. McLaggan stops.

"I'm sorry," she says. "I should have said something about the smell. I didn't want to frighten you."

"It's all right."

"You see, Mr. Lewis, my grandson, he's going to die. You'll think I'm a cruel woman, that he should be in hospital, and you'd be right to think it. But he's been there, you see, been there for eighteen months. I'd heard of psoriasis before, I knew sadness and worry and so on could make it worse. But I didn't know it could get this bad."

She grabs Paul's arm.

"Mr. Lewis, he *wanted* to come home. He knew what it meant to leave there, but he *wanted* to come home."

OUTSIDE, IT IS nearly dark. Lights have come on in the houses, and in the square the vendors' stalls are gone. He walks slowly through the gathering dusk. At the ends of the streets he passes, views open of sky and water, shelves of cloud floating on the horizon.

In the room at the hotel, Ellen is waiting for him. She's been crying, he can see, but has stopped now. She doesn't have the same alarmed expression she had yesterday. She's gotten their bags out and some of their clothes are folded inside.

For a few minutes they don't speak.

"I asked at the desk about the schedule," she says finally. "We can get a train in the morning."

"What about the letters you came for?"

She glances up at him. He's never seen her look this exhausted before.

"I've seen them," she says. She sits perched on the edge of the bed, her hands folded on her lap. The way she gestured: that was one of the things he fell in love with. Her hands would turn open, fingers spread, her arms moving in quick arcs and circles, energy that seemed to him miraculous.

"I'm sorry," is all he can think to say.

She kneels on the floor and starts packing the rest of their belongings, tears streaming down her face.

IT IS IN the middle of the night that he wakes and goes to sit by the window. The hotel is quiet and there is no traffic on the street. He can hear the steady, washing sound of the sea and he imagines the blankness of night out there in the northern waters.

Once, when he was a boy, his parents took him on a cruise ship, and after dinner one night his father and he stood on the deck, and Paul imagined what it would be like if he were to fall, disappearing into that vast, anonymous darkness. He can still remember how his heart thumped in his chest, how he clung to that railing that separated him from death.

Who could say all that has happened since then, or why?

As a man, he has pictured his own end so many times the thought arrives like an old friend, there to reassure him.

For an hour or more he sits, listening to the water. He is

calm as he goes to the desk; calm, as he writes his note to Ellen.

I've been a burden long enough. I hope eventually you will remember the better times. Please forgive me.

A TAXI PICKS them up after breakfast and takes them to the station. They board the front car of the train, storing their luggage on a rack by the door, and then they find a compartment to themselves.

The overhead speaker announces the train will be held in the station for ten minutes, just as the schedule that Paul checked said it would.

Ellen roots in her handbag for something. Paul clutches the envelope in his pocket.

As she bends forward, her hair, parted in the middle, comes loose from behind her ears. He washed that velvet black hair the week they married, lying in the tub in her apartment, lathering her head as it rested on his chest. They would have three children, she said. There would be closets of toys and winter coats and summer holidays and a home to return to.

Enough, he thinks, and stops remembering. In Dr. Gormley's waiting room, the coatrack would still persist. The beige watercooler. The dog-eared magazines. The humming. The air without scent. He sees Ellen, alone, walking the aisle of a supermarket, pausing, taking a can from the shelf. He feels incredibly tired.

From the window, Paul watches as the last of the passengers board at the far end of the platform. The rumble of the engine grows louder. He stands and bends down to kiss Ellen's cheek.

"I'm just going to use the bathroom," he says, and then can't help adding, "You'll be all right."

"Sure," she says distractedly, examining their tickets.

He moves quickly down the passageway. At the end of the car, he takes his bag from the rack and steps off the train. The conductor is standing there on the platform.

"There's a woman in number twelve," Paul says to him. "Could you give her this?"

The conductor takes the envelope from him with no apparent interest.

"I'll see she gets it," he says, putting the whistle between his lips.

MRS. MCLAGGAN IS just returning from the shops as he enters the lane. She does not notice him until he is there at the door.

"Mr. Lewis," she says, glancing down at his bag. "You've come for a visit. How good of you, Albert will be so pleased."

Again there is the high, rotting odor as they step into the hall, the terrier trailing behind. In the kitchen, he watches Mrs. McLaggan take her tins and vegetables from her cloth bag.

"Colder this morning," she says. "The haar will be here soon. You won't be able to see a thing in a day or two for all the mist and fog."

The groceries put in place, she fills the kettle at the sink. "Albert enjoyed that yesterday, really he did."

"How do you manage?" Paul asks. "Knowing he's going to die."

She arranges milk and sugar on a tray.

"It'll sound odd, I know, but the idea's not so peculiar to me actually. I used to nurse on a ward, you see. Before you were born, dear, during the war. They were desperate for people. Adverts up in all the shops about how the young women had to come south. I'd never been. A hospital outside Southampton's where they put me. We got the ones who weren't going back. Most were healthy enough, just lost a leg or an arm . . . There were others, though, dying ones. Not much to do for them really but keep them comfortable if you could. Some of the nurses, they were young, you see—we all were—and they would tell the dying ones things would be fine. But I have to say, Mr. Lewis, I couldn't bring myself to reassure them like that. Struck me as a lie."

She pours boiling water into the pot.

"The beds had wheels on. After the doctors' rounds I'd roll the sicker ones up next to each other so they could talk. They were just glad someone else knew, I think."

The kettle is rinsed and set back on the counter.

Once again, they ascend the stairs, Mrs. McLaggan carrying the tray. Albert is asleep, his red face turned to one side on the pillow. Mrs. McLaggan sets the tray down on the side table.

"I'll leave you with him now," she says, laying a hand on Paul's shoulder.

When she has gone, he perches on the stool by the bed. Here, he can make out the boy's features hidden beneath the rotting skin: the thin lips and pointed nose, the bony forehead of his Celtic ancestors, the corners of his skull showing at the temples. Paul lets the stench rise up into his nostrils, breathing it in freely.

It will not be long now, he thinks, for either of them.

The boy's head moves slightly on the pillow and he wakes.

"Would you like to hear another story?" Paul asks.

Albert nods. It is not thanks Paul sees in his expression but forgiveness.

"Tell me about the kings."

REUNION

WHEN IT FINALLY arrived, the minister's letter came in a typed envelope bearing no return address. It was signed at the bottom in careful script. The request had been seen to, the arrangements made. The local council would require a check; an address was given. James read it on the stairs up to his flat. When he'd found his keys and got inside, he put the letter on the mantel to make sure he wouldn't forget.

Simon, his manager at the estate agents, had initially thought it odd that James should want his holiday at such short notice, and all four weeks at once. But it was midsummer, nothing selling, the time as good as any. He'd said James could leave right away if all his work was in order, which it was—he had seen to that before making his request. He stood now in his living room, removing from his briefcase the bits and pieces he had collected from his desk, placing the framed picture of his father on the side table.

"How 'bout a drink before you head off?" his redheaded colleague, Patrick, had offered. He had been kind and helpful from the beginning, yet James was caught off guard by his suggestion, a first in their yearlong acquaintance. What would he have to say, sitting in a pub with this fellow he'd spent time thinking about? Over the partition, colleagues had looked on. "Perhaps another time," was all James had managed to respond.

The groceries put away, he showered, and afterward stood before the mirror, wrapped in a towel. Three or four times he drew the razor over the taut flesh of his chin before he was satisfied the stubble was gone. Shaving made him look younger than twenty-five; with his hair cut the right way he could still pass for a university student. He examined the skin beneath his eyes, noticing a little flaking, the hint of a rash just below the surface. As he stepped back from the mirror, the latter disappeared, and he observed his smooth face with a modicum of contentment; not so bad, he thought.

In his bedroom, he found a clean T-shirt and pair of boxers, folded neatly in the bureau drawer. The room, as usual, was tidy: the bed made, the curtains fastened in place, laundry piled in the corner hamper. He returned his suit to its hanger, fitted his brogues with shoehorns, and put his tie on the rack fixed to the inside of the wardrobe door, wondering, all the while, how long this order would last.

ACROSS THE COMMON, kids scurried over the public courts, swatting at tennis balls that arced slowly in the damp air. Along the perimeter, people jogged on the asphalt path. James crossed the green, headed toward a line of trees whose branches swayed against a darkening sky. There was food in the refrigerator, he reminded himself, and a guide to the evening's television awaiting him should he lose his nerve. Beneath the trees, he took a seat on a bench. The occasional car passed behind on the far side of the stone wall that surrounded the common. Music from an open window rose and fell on the wind, losing itself in the hushing sound of the trees. A couple, hand in hand, walked along the park's edge. Just off the Underground, their briefcases weighed heavily in their hands; his tie was loosened, she wore sneakers. James watched as they disappeared through the gate, headed for the warren of row houses that stretched over south London toward the river.

It was seven-thirty, the light beginning to go, and parents were collecting their children from the football pitch. Nearby, a gardener stowed tools in the municipal shed before padlocking the door behind him. A middle-aged woman in evening dress hurried a terrier over the edge of the grass, pulling it back toward the lights of the houses, visible now through the gate's arch.

James opened his letter pad and began to write on the small, lined sheets:

Dear Father,

Today I left my job at Shipley's. We've been doing very little business, and they won't miss me. This isn't for lack of effort on my part. I've worked long days and made lot of calls, but the market is bad just now and no one has made a sale in three weeks. My manager was helpful and said I could take my holidays straightaway. The hardest thing was saying good-bye to Patrick, the fellow I've told you about. We'd become quite friendly, he even asked me for a drink this evening, but I was afraid of what I might have been tempted to say. I don't suppose he notices my glances at the office. This must all seem rather odd to you, worrying about the young man across the desk. At my age, you'd already married Mum. I wonder what you really make of it.

He could just make out the words on the page when the streetlamp across the wall came on. He closed the pad and returned it to his pocket. The common was dark. Above the faint glow of the city rose the lighted towers of the housing estates at Sand's End. The distant sound of traffic crossing the river floated toward him over the grass, making the space before him seem vast, the darkness rolling in quiet waves up to his feet. A few minutes passed before he heard the first steps on the path, slow and intermittent. Then to his left, a shape moving through the trees, catching the corner of his eye, vanishing as he turned to look. The streetlamp felt like a spotlight now, blinding him to the darkened house. He unzipped his jacket and put his hands in the pockets of his jeans. A light flickered by the hedge beside the tennis courts, lit the tip of a cigarette, and was gone, leaving behind the glow of an ember. James felt his breathing become shallow; he dropped his shoulders and told himself to relax. Here and there leaves were brushed aside by shuffling feet. Rising from the bench, he headed for the small copse beyond the gardener's shed, impatient for his eyes to adjust to the lack of light. He leant against a tree, training all his senses on the darkness. Nearby, a man groaned softly. From over the wall, music still floated.

Several minutes passed before he sensed a figure approaching. As the man came closer, James saw he was wearing a suit, his tie pulled down from the collar of a white shirt. Late thirties, James guessed quickly, unsure whether to advance or retreat. The visage emerged from shadow—a broad neck, double chin, the features of a once handsome boy cloaked in the flesh of a man's face. Their eyes had met and James already felt with paranoid terror the disappointment he would inflict were he to step away now. The man attempted a half smile, generous and disarming. James cast his eyes to the ground. The hand on his shoulder came as a surprise, but he fell into the touch, making of the man's extended arm an embrace.

Afterward, walking home, the air felt cold against his face. His breath became full again and he jogged the two blocks from the gate to his front door. On the stairs, he felt lightheaded, as though all of a sudden his blood had gone thin, and he took the last flight more slowly.

A WEEK PASSED. On Tuesday, the office called about a semidetached in Parson's Green; they couldn't find the paperwork. James let the machine answer and phoned back the next morning. How was the holiday going? Simon asked. Where had he gone off to? A village in Cornwall, James said, just a bed-and-breakfast, a quick walk to the sea. Wonderful to have time on his own.

Matinees were cheaper than evening shows and London was full of movie houses. He watched the films he had missed over the last few months, soon moving back further in time to the repertory houses—seventies classics, the Italian directors, the films of Dirk Bogarde. If he rose at eleven, had a leisurely breakfast, and chose a long picture, the matinee would consume most of the afternoon, and evening would soon be upon him. He cooked at home and visited the common at night. Each evening, as he sat on the bench waiting for the light to fade, he wrote a letter to his father, even if it was only a few lines, being sure to place it in an envelope as soon as he returned to the flat.

One Friday night he arrived home from the cinema to discover the fridge was empty; he had seen a double feature, and it was now past closing time. Just as happy not to have to cook, he showered and changed before heading out for a curry.

The place was crammed with an after-work crowd that had stayed for supper and was getting progressively drunker. He sat on his own at a table near the kitchen, reading the newspaper. Just as his food arrived, he heard a voice behind him.

"Is that you, Finn?" He turned around and saw a broad-faced male of his own age, his complexion brightened with alcohol, leering down at him. "Clive Newman, from Stockwell, you remember—football in the fog." Without waiting for confirmation, he went on. "Crazy coincidence, hey? I'm back for just a week, Hong Kong—banking—and Trisha's here too, girlfriend of mine. Why don't you come over then, Jamie? That's it, right? Jamie?"

"James."

"Right. Eat with us," he instructed, lifting the dish of rice from James's table and heading for his own. What could he do? He picked up the rest of his food and moved reluctantly to the front of the restaurant, where a group of seven or eight sat around a table covered with beer glasses.

"Everyone! We have here Stockwell's finest actor—*H.M.S. Pinafore,* wasn't it, Finn?" A few of the assembled chuckled absently while the others continued to chat. Someone had passed his tandoori down the table and a young woman in pearls and lipstick was picking at it with a fork.

"Did we order this?" she asked.

"Actually . . . ," James began, but Clive had his arm around him and had begun to speak.

"Have you ever been back, Finn? I was there last year—Old Boys' Day—cricket versus the school side and all that. For a prep school they do quite a job—tents, speeches—the whole routine. None of the fellows showed up, though, just a pack of geezers." The table's food arrived and people began spooning the oily mixtures onto their plates. "Where do the years go, hey? Lost there somewhere."

Despite himself, James's mind wandered back: chapped legs in winter; the mud-soaked parquet of the basement changing rooms.

"It's all ahead of us," Clive Newman said. "Christ, we're only a quarter century old, aren't we, my angel?"

"Yeah," the girl sitting next to James said, appearing not to have heard the question. Trisha was an ethereal-looking character with a mass of hair as light as the skin of her face. Her eyes were large and protruding, as though she were forever alarmed. James thought them an unlikely couple.

"Are you in business too, then?" she asked in a soft voice, beneath the rising chatter of another round of drinks. She was speaking to James alone, removing Clive from the conversation with the quietness of her tone. Clive turned to his food and was soon caught up in discussion with a man sitting across the table.

"Well," James began, "at the moment I don't do much of anything."

"Do you enjoy that?" she asked, apparently uninterested in the whys and wherefores.

"I can't say I do."

"Me neither." She looked down the table, sizing up the young woman in pearls, whose shiny brown hair hung in a gentle curl to her shoulders. Over the cacophony of deeper, male voices, this woman's nasal inflection rose. The accent was well-to-do, the repartee with her male companions conducted with nonchalance, perhaps a little disdain. Trisha looked down again, inspecting her hand of painted nails, pressing back strands of frayed cuticle with the edge of her thumbnail.

"I take it you're not working at the moment," James said.

She laughed. Pushing her plate away untouched, she fiddled with a pack of cigarettes. Her smile stiffened, came to pieces, and appeared again, as though attached to strings pulled by other hands. Then she leaned in closer to James and said even more quietly than before, "This isn't as it appears. I'm here in what you might call a professional capacity. Your friend Clive wanted a little company while he's in town. I think he's an asshole. But if he stays conscious I guess we'll be sleeping together in a few hours." She sat up again in her chair and smiled vaguely at Clive, whose bloated face had grown redder with drink.

"You can laugh at me now," she said nervously, out of the corner of her mouth. Then she turned to James again, pulled in by the intensity of her thought. "You can go ahead and tell me what a worthless life this is." Her whole expression reached forward in anticipation, as if she saw a blow to the head coming and was determined not to flinch.

James felt as if he had been yanked from a stupor, pulled

into the tight space of this woman's fury, and to his surprise he didn't feel like turning away.

"No," he said, "I don't want to say that. Honestly."

She leaned her elbow on the table, resting her head on her hand. She looked disappointed. Around the table people were calling and laughing, conversation having given way to anecdotes shouted over the din.

"So are you rich or something?" she asked beneath the noise. "Is that why you've got time on your hands?" Gathering her plate back, she picked at a piece of bread.

"No," James replied, feeling a sudden tenderness for this stranger. "To tell you the truth, I'm dying."

The girl froze for an instant, torn from her own form of complacency. His words seemed to filter through her mind, her expression passing from confusion to incredulity to a kind of somber calm.

"I'm sorry," she said, and James thought it genuine. "Do you have long?"

He looked into her large black eyes, then down at his hands.

"Difficult to say. Probably not."

She was the first person he'd told. A year and a half the medications had worked, and then suddenly they were no good. A resistant strain, the doctors said. For a moment, he felt again the devouring shame that he'd let this disease he'd been so warned of into his body, let it in because he wanted pleasure and somewhere along the way believed people he shouldn't have. But he'd learned early in life there were things it was best not to think about. The shame passed and he didn't let his mind pursue it.

Suddenly, Clive was leaning over them, putting his arms around their shoulders, his bulbous face inserted between them.

"What are you two going on about?" he said, louder than necessary. "Just here a week, Finn, want to see my girl." He cupped Trisha's head in his hand and kissed her roughly on the lips. "Go on then, push over." James moved down a seat. Over Clive's shoulder, the girl looked at him and for a moment he felt his tenderness reflected in the concern of her gaze. Clive began to caress her cheek. She managed to smile at him before closing her eyes.

Later, standing in the restaurant's foyer as the group prepared to leave, Clive insisted James join them all the next evening at a pub on the King's Road. Laughton, another classmate, would be along. James muttered an excuse—a project at work, long hours.

As she leaned against Clive by the cigarette machine, the girl came no higher than his shoulder.

"It was good to meet you," James said but a waiter glided between them and when he'd passed, the girl had looked away; repetition would seem overbearing, he thought. He waved good-bye, and ahead of the others, made his way out of the restaurant.

On the curb in front of him a bus pulled alongside the shelter, and a small group of passengers stepped off the rear platform, disbanding as they gained the pavement. He headed east, behind the quickly disappearing figures.

THE BENCH BY the wall of the common was empty, the street-lamp already on. He should go home, he told himself. But then there was a rustling of feet by the beech hedge, the sound of shallow breath. He kept walking. At the copse, he saw an unshaven man in a tank top picking his way carefully around the glimmer of the ground's muddy patches. James moved farther toward the shed and waited just in from the path. Men, young and old, wandered among the trees, stopping now and again to pierce the shadow, a white piece of clothing or the whites of their determined eyes catching a speck of lamplight and floating for an instant in the darkness. He let them pass by, trying still to convince himself, as he always tried, that he would thank himself for turning away.

Soon a man with thinning black hair, wearing a suit and polished shoes, approached and hung beside him. James remained still, reminding himself to breathe. There were muffled greetings, a hand placed flat on his beating chest. He reached out to loosen the man's tie, and then their lips met. James closed his eyes and the pent welter of longing rushed into his limbs. He ran his hands down the man's back, pressed his shoulders, grabbed at the back of his head. In the now perfect darkness, he had the oddest sensation it was the girl from the restaurant he was embracing, her slender frame, her plight. He moved more gently, holding her like he would hold an old person, or someone who has lost their strength, trying to forgive by the way he touched. Then he felt the scratch of stubble along his neck, ran his hand past the dangling tie, and it was no longer the girl he was pressed against in this dance of apparitions, but his father. The hands at the fly, the condom, the warm mouth, they all came as a disappointment.

ONE MORNING A month later, a man from British Telecom knocked on the door. For weeks, James had thrown his post in the garbage unopened and the habit seemed to be attracting unsolicited visits. They had sent warnings, the man said, they had tried to contact him by phone, but his service had now been disconnected. Was there a problem? He told James there were installment plans for people with financial difficulties.

"It's not the money," James said. "I don't want a phone."

The man looked confused, as though perhaps James were a disturbed character and the service under discussion that of a halfway home. He peered through the front window, presumably looking for the person in charge.

The previous Tuesday, the cable service had gone out, and soon thereafter, James had noticed that the newspaper no longer appeared on the doorstep each morning. Stepping into a taxi on the way to a cinema one afternoon, he had seen two men in sunglasses knocking at his door, and recognized them as employees of the collection agency Shipley's used for its rental properties. They must do a sideline in credit cards, he'd thought, for while he ignored his mail, he had been careful to pay his rent.

"Here," James said to the man as he picked up the telephone, which he had wrapped up in its cords and placed at the foot of the stairs a week before, "I imagine you've come for this."

THAT EVENING, AS the light faded over the common, he wrote:

Dear Father,

We are well past the summer solstice now and the days are getting shorter. I suppose it's with this sort of observation a letter should begin, in the safety of neutral facts.

Since I've stopped working, time has slowed. I think a lot about the past, and the memories tend to make the present less real, like the memory of you standing at the back door in your blue suit, leaning your head against the stone as dusk encompassed the yard. Some days I feel as though I am still in that yard, watching you, wondering what you're thinking. Do you see me there? Do you remember?

You will be glad to know I've been responsible about my money. Everything's been drawn up and signed. Mum should have no problem with it. I find you now and again here on the common, bits and pieces of you scattered in the woods, but as the days go by, so the need lessens. I'll be coming home soon.

He remained seated at the end of the bench, listening to the trees and the music from the flat behind. His breath was shallow, though not from excitement. In the vestibule, his hands shook as he held his key to the lock, and he had to steady himself against the wall. On the stairs, he made good use of the banister.

IT WAS A rainy morning later that week when the doorbell rang again. Wary of the bill collectors, James looked through the curtain to identify the visitor. It was Patrick, his colleague from Shipley's. James was supposed to have returned to work five days ago, but by that time he'd unplugged the phone. If they had been trying to call, he knew nothing of it. He considered letting the doorbell ring, pretending to be away, but his nerve gave out and he went round to the hall. Patrick stood in the doorway in a raincoat, his red hair clustered into dark strands by the rain.

"James! You're here!" he bellowed. "What's the story, mate? We thought you were dead down a ditch somewhere."

James stood staring at this young man over whom he had fretted so during his year at the office, catering, invisibly, to his whims and preferences, whims and preferences James had likely imagined to begin with—an elaborate set of spinning wheels, attached to nothing.

He hadn't spoken to anyone in over a week and found himself caught off guard by Patrick's presence, as though this person ought to have moved on by now, the way a thought passes from the mind. But there he was, dripping rain, a dopey half smile playing across his face.

"Come in," James said.

Patrick hesitated, glancing at James in his bathrobe and slippers, unshaven, sensing, it appeared, that he'd wandered into something larger than expected. "Simon was worried," he said. In the twilight of the hall, he narrowed his eyes. "You don't look so great. Have you been sick?"

"Yeah. This rash, I . . . It won't go away. I've had a head cold too. I was going to call but there was some problem with the phones—in the building, I mean."

Patrick was looking through to the living room, taking in the clothes strewn on the furniture, the mantel cluttered with jars of ointment and old prescription bottles.

"As a matter of fact, I won't be coming back to the office. I'm moving."

"What's this, then? Does Simon know?"

"No. I should tell him. You see, I've decided I need to spend some time with my family, so I'm not going to stay on here. It's a bit sudden, I know." He felt himself balking at the ruse and yet beneath that feeling was a relief, an unsentimental farewell to the bond of simple honesty, to the assumptions they might ever have shared. He had occupied himself with the idea of this man's happiness and now he could cast at him a distant glance, fiddling with the truth.

"Pardon me, I should have taken your coat," James said, suddenly all politeness. "Won't you come in and sit down?"

"I should be getting back." His expression grew confused, the expression of a man who has wandered into the wrong cinema and finds himself in the dark with strange or disturbing images.

Before he knew what he had done, James had his hand on Patrick's cheek and was passing his thumb over the soft, freckled skin beneath his eye. "Thank you," he said, "thank you for everything."

Blushing, Patrick turned his head away and reached back for the handle of the door. "I must go."

He stepped down the walk to the gate and didn't turn back on the street but kept moving until he had disappeared behind the bus shelter and was gone.

JAMES DIDN'T CALL Simon. At first, he harbored a feeling of guilt, a worry he had let someone down, but as the weeks went by, his sense of the world became ever more abstract. He began to doubt that if he went to the office there would be anyone there he recognized, or who would recognize him. The doctors had said this could happen, one's memory might go, confusions could overtake you as the virus entered the brain.

Slowly, time began to evaporate, the process swallowing whole periods of his life. He forgot Simon and the office, Patrick and the year he had spent worrying over his affections. One morning he no longer recognized the flat he was occupying and began to imagine that the real occupant might return and send him onto the street. He wandered about the unfamiliar rooms, thinking at times that he was in the yard of his childhood, crouched by the birdbath, where he would wait as dusk fell.

There was a common nearby and he would walk there in the evening. Often, as he approached the far corner, where a bench sat empty in lamplight, he would feel nonplussed. From somewhere would come a barely audible whisper, one that vanished as soon as he stopped to listen, as a dream vanishes beneath the effort of recollection.

Returning from his walk one evening he was accosted by a young woman. It was by the pedestrian crossing. She had just come over the road and was about to pass by when she came to a halt before him and looked intently at his face. She had the overlarge eyes of a lizard and a gaunt face that matched the color of her hair. She began to speak to James, asking him questions about his health, exclaiming how much weight he had lost. Did he need money? she asked. He smiled and answered the questions as best he could, hoping she would continue on her way. He had seen her at a bad time, she said, riffling through her bag to find a cigarette; things were different now, she was out of all that racket. He nodded in agreement, and this seemed to comfort her, for her hands ceased to move so rapidly, and she placed one briefly on his arm. She was sorry about everything, she said, she hadn't meant to bother him about herself. Was there nothing she could do? Politely, he declined, imagining she had mistaken him for someone else.

JAMES SAT IN a room by a window trying to read a book. It was afternoon, and outside a steady rain fell. The novel was about an old man who captivated his grandson with stories of his ancestors, drawing closer and closer to the present, until finally he was telling the boy the story of the boy's own life, and the narrative became a prophecy that frightened the listener. He read a few pages at a time, resting his eyes now and again, or just staring out onto the street. There, shawled women queued for the bus and old men with their caps pulled down hung in doorways, waiting for the rain to pass. Their silhouettes appeared fuzzy, blurred by the weather, their dark shoes blending with the wet pavement until it seemed to James as though they were sinking in mud. He shook his head a bit and returned his attention to the page. But he had lost his place in the story and he found himself reading the same sentences over and over until the words made no sense at all. He put the book down and, looking out, was transfixed by what he saw: his father standing across the street, gazing up at the window. He was in his blue suit, his arms hanging straight at his sides, the corners of his mouth turned down. Motionless, he stared at James, who felt as though heavy cables were being cast from the sockets of his father's eyes over the street and through the window until they wrapped themselves around his skull. He rushed to the window and put his hands against the pane, but when he looked again, the figure was gone, dissolved into the rectangles of concrete and the soot-stained wall behind.

It was later that day that he fainted, standing over the sink with a glass of water in his hand. He saw the counter begin to move quickly to one side, then blackness. When he came around he was lying on his back on the linoleum floor. The room was dark, and by the projection of car headlights sloping across the ceiling, he could tell it was dark outside as well. He lay there awhile, listening to the cars pass, and farther off the sound of jumbo jets descending to earth. When he moved to rise, he found he had no strength in his arms, and shifting about on the hard floor, realized he was lying in a pool of sweat. For a moment, panic gripped him and he felt he might scream. But just as it had arisen, so it passed, and he stared again at the sloping lights on the ceiling. Gently, images flowed before his mind, and the inscrutable enormity of remembered life washed back over him, leaving him weightless and expectant. He thought of Stockwell, and the exhilaration he had felt on winter afternoons when games were through, running back over the fields to where the parents waited in their heated cars. And he thought of his sealed letters gathered on the living room shelf. He was calm. Soon he would be home again, resting beside his father's grave, just as the minister's letter had promised.

DIVINATION

ON THE FOOTBALL pitch, daylight had begun to fade. The other boys were inside already. Samuel had stayed on the field half an hour to practice penalty kicks with his friend Giles, who stood now in front of the goal, waiting for another shot to come. Samuel took ten steps back, then ran at the ball, kicking it high and to the left, missing to the outside by a foot or two.

"Shall we pack it in?" Giles said, dragging his foot across the grass to clear off the mud.

"Don't you want to have a go?"

Giles shook his head. "I'm knackered, let's go in."

It was as they were walking back toward the old manor house the school occupied that Samuel became aware of the cooing and flapping of wings inside the crumbling dovecote, the muffled sounds echoing over the lawn. At that moment, for no apparent reason, he thought: How sad that Jevins should die now, like this, alone in his apartment over the sixth-form dormitories.

Mr. Jevins, who had stood over them just that morning in his gown and oval glasses, reciting Latin—by whom, or what it meant, none of them knew. They'd discovered if they set the wall clock forward ten minutes and rang Bennet's alarm, Jevins, half deaf, would imagine the sound to be the bell and let them go early. Eighty he must have been, or older. His voice a gravelly whisper, only now and then rising to a pitch, on about some emperor or battle, Samuel guessed. Boys ignored him freely, chatting and throwing paper. Ever since he'd come to Saint Gilbert's, Samuel had felt a pain associated with this man, a feeling he couldn't articulate or conceive. This morning for the first time Jevins had slammed his leather book down on the windowsill and with a strain shouted, "Do you boys want me to continue with this lesson or not!"

The thug Miller had stood up and addressed the class. "Proposition on the floor, gentlemen. Do we want Jevins to continue with the lesson? Show of hands for the nays."

Most of the boys had raised their hands, covering their

mouths and tittering. Jevins had just stood there and watched. Then Bennet's alarm clock had rung and the boys had begun stuffing their satchels and heading for the door. Samuel was slow gathering his books; he'd been trying to study for a geography quiz. When he looked up, the room had emptied, except for Mr. Jevins, still at his post. He'd been a foot soldier in World War II, they said, shot off the beach at Dunkirk and sent back over the channel on D-Day. The wrinkled skin beneath his eyes twitched, a tic of the nerves, the expression of defeat unchanged as he stared at his last remaining pupil. Samuel had grabbed his satchel and run from the room.

Walking now, back from the playing fields through the dusk with Giles, Samuel could see lights on in the library, where the upper-form boarders would be studying for their entrance exams. At the top of the building he could see the lights still on in Mr. Jevins's apartment, the curtains pulled. For a moment he wondered if the old man lay shut-eyed on the bed or in the green leather chair in his front room, where he'd sat two autumns ago elaborating the rules for the new boarders: how to treat matrons, whom to speak to if there were difficulties—deputy prefect, then a prefect, and only then a master. It felt wrong trying to picture where his teacher's body lay, as if he'd come upon Mr. Jevins in his pants in the upstairs hall at some odd hour, an embarrassing thing he wouldn't soon forget.

In the courtyard, before Samuel could decide whether to say anything, Giles turned off into the changing rooms for Lincoln House. Samuel kept walking on toward his own dorm. When he entered the main hall after showering and eating supper, he saw Mr. Kinnet, the new master, smoking a cigarette at the window by the door to the library. He had night duty this week and was watching the study hall. Samuel wanted to tell him what had happened to Jevins. Someone should know, he thought, an adult.

"Got a problem there, Phipps? Need to use the loo or something?"

"No, sir."

"You look as if you've been sick."

"Just tired, sir."

"It's barely half seven, shouldn't you be off being terrorized by your superiors?"

"It's Friday, sir. Most of them have gone home."

"Make friends with the day boys, that's my advice. Some local tosser with a big house and a pool. Get his mum to drag you home on weekends."

He extinguished his cigarette by reaching out the window and mashing it against the iron casement.

"Mr. Jevins," Samuel blurted. "It's a pity."

"What's that, Phipps?"

"Nothing." He walked quickly up the front stairs, their creaking awful and loud, and then up the next flight to the landing and along into his dorm. The room was empty. From the window he looked back across the darkened lawn. He wished he were with Trevor, his older brother. He felt an aching kind of sadness, but right away a voice in his head told him not to be a weakling.

Though it wouldn't be lights-out for another hour, he climbed into bed. He read three geography lessons that weren't due until Monday and worked over figures in his chemistry lab book, doing the sums in his head, putting a mark next to each figure he'd recalculated. The Latin textbook he left on the shelf behind him, wondering, despite himself, how long it would take them to find a new teacher and whether the old man had suffered as he went.

"PHIPPSY! OY!"

Giles was shaking him awake. It was long before breakfast but all the boys were up and out of bed.

"Jevins croaked! They're carrying him down right now! The ambulance's right out front! Bennet's been crying for ages, the wus. Come on—get up!"

Samuel ran to the window, wriggling between taller boys to get a view. There were no sirens or flashing lights. The ambulance looked almost abandoned sitting in the empty gravel car park, its back doors hanging open, its headlights on though the sun had already peeked over the lip of the field.

" 'Bout time," some little second-former said. "He was bloody ancient."

"Younger than your mother's twat, Krishorn."

Silence fell as two men dressed in navy blue jackets and trousers emerged from the portico with a stretcher held between them, on it a long mound of a shape covered over with a sheet, the body too wide for the conveyance, arms rolled out to the side, hands visible. Bennet's weeping could be heard from the back of the room. The lead man stepped up into the van and the stretcher disappeared from sight.

"No deus ex machina for Jevins, hey? Plot over." Giles stared at the ambulance with a wistful look, as if he were staring at his parents' car pulling out of the drive. Samuel gripped the cool stone of the window frame, the sounds around him seeming to fade from his ears.

At breakfast, the headmaster stood up from the head table and said he had a sad bit of news. Mr. Jevins had died of a heart attack the previous evening. "He served this school for forty-two years and was the finest teacher of Latin I have ever known." At this, a few snickers. With reproving emphasis, the headmaster went on, "And *just* so as there won't be any idle talk on the subject, it was Mrs. Pebbly who found Mr. Jevins at rest in his rooms this morning. There will be a service in chapel Monday at four. Your parents are being notified. Out of respect for Mr. Jevins I think it fitting we eat the remainder of our breakfast in silence." And with that he sat down.

THAT AFTERNOON, SAMUEL tried watching Giles and a few others play a game of French cricket out by the field house, but his gaze kept wandering up to the billowing white clouds. The sight of the stretcher, the clean white sheet, the open palms. It had stilled a part of Samuel's mind he'd never realized had been moving. A tiny ball in the middle of his brain had spun to a halt. It scared him. He'd always thought fear would be something fast, a thing that pushed you forward.

Up in the dorm that morning after breakfast, he'd still hoped for an explanation of his knowing, a conversation between masters he'd overheard without realizing, some comment made at supper. But when the headmaster had described what happened, the timing of it, all of a sudden Samuel saw the food on his plate and the boys opposite him and the whole dining hall as if through the wrong end of a telescope. It was as though the everyday world, all that was familiar to him, had been revealed as a tiny, crowded dwelling, full of noise and chatter. A house on an empty plain. Beyond its walls a vast landscape.

The barely noticeable pace of the clouds' approach across the sky seemed like evidence of this hidden enormity, his classmates' frantic motions on the pitch nothing but the buzzing of insects against the window of an attic room. Sitting there on the playing fields, he longed more ardently than he ever had to be with Trevor, hanging out in his room, watching him at his desk fiddling with his computer, talking on and on about computer things, the books he'd ordered by mail open beside him, his brother not listening to half of whatever Samuel said, but nodding. His brother who'd never seemed happy at his own school, who never seemed to make friends. In that room with Trevor, he might still be safe.

By the time his parents' Peugeot turned into the car park at ten to four on the Monday, it seemed he hadn't spoken to another person in years. He ran to the car. His mother in her black dress and handbag had barely risen from the passenger's seat when he began, "Mum, I knew, I knew before everyone else, before they told us, I knew they'd have to get another teacher and it was right when it happened, just after seven, I knew he was dead before anyone."

He burst into tears, pressing his face against his mother's

body, hugging her. Her hands came down to rub his back, arms cradling his head.

"All right, dear, it's all right."

"But I knew," he mumbled into her dress. "Why? Why?"

Her hands came to a stop and she pressed him harder against her.

"It's okay now, it'll be all right . . . Of course you didn't know, dear. He was a good teacher . . . you liked him. It's hard, that's all."

Samuel looked up into her face. She had long black hair a bit ruffled now in the breeze. She never usually wore makeup but today she'd put on pale lipstick, the look in her eyes the look she had when he got sick. He wanted to comfort her, to explain.

"Mum, I knew on Friday. Mrs. Pebbly didn't find him till Saturday morning."

She smiled weakly, looking down at the gravel.

"You remember when Granny died," his father said across the top of the car, his voice weirdly loud. He was staring intently at Samuel, his shirt and tie done tightly up against his throat. "You remember we were all sad then. You're sad now. You see? And sometimes you think things when you're sad. It's natural."

"But it was Friday. I was playing—"

His father turned his head away abruptly, glancing across the field. He closed his mouth and swallowed, his eyes squinting into the distance, lips turning down into a kind of grimace, as if he were forcing something nasty tasting down his throat.

"Come on," he said to Samuel's mother, turning around and heading across the lot. "We'll be late."

In the chapel, the headmaster recounted Mr. Jevins's life, his days in the army, a military cross, teaching in Rhodesia, the years of service to Saint Gilbert's. His elderly sister said a few words. The ceremony ended with a recorded playing of Jevins's favorite church music, Allegri's *Miserere.* The boarders all knew it, having heard the recording the third Sunday of every month, when the old man had doubled as minister. Each time he played the song, he reminded them that the Latin sung was Psalm Fifty-one, which he would recite to them afterward in English. Samuel remembered vividly him standing on the step of the altar in his gown, the only master left who wore one. He would pause in his reading before the last line of the penultimate verse, his voice dropping so low it seemed as if he were talking to himself: *The sacrifice acceptable to God is a broken spirit; a broken and contrite heart, O God, thou wilt not despise.*

No one translated for the audience after the singing ended. Boys and their parents filed from the chapel into the courtyard. The women from the kitchen removed cling wrap from platters of sandwiches and began pouring the tea.

MR. JEVINS HAD died only a month into the school year. The headmaster conducted the Latin classes until Christmas, doing a poor job of hiding his shock at how little the students had been taught. After the holiday, there was a new man, younger than Kinnet he looked, and not easily fooled.

By the time Samuel came home for the summer, his parents appeared to have forgotten his teacher's death, as though it were just another term-time event, a cricket match won or lost. He spent a week lying around the house, then at last Trevor returned.

He was sixteen now, five years older than Samuel. He seemed taller and thinner than he had at Christmas, his acne a bit worse. Usually when they returned from school they would spend at least a few hours rigging traps for the cat, books pulled off tables by strings soaked in tuna water or obstacle courses of cosmetics items taken from their mother's cupboard and arranged on the stairs. But each holiday Trevor seemed less interested and this time he didn't want to do it at all.

He'd got his learner's permit and three mornings a week he had driving lessons. The rest of his time he spent in his room at the computer, programming in some machine code, the screen covered in lines of numbers and symbols. Newsletters from American software companies and product literature covered his desk and floor. Samuel watched his brother work, or just hung out in his room and read or played on the game station.

It didn't matter that Trevor only half listened to him or that when he did listen he often made fun of him. His brother being there, the sound of his voice, it was enough. The distance from things he'd kept experiencing during the year, that odd retreat from the physical world, it diminished with Trevor around. Lying on the floor beneath his brother's window, staring up at the sky on those summer afternoons, listening to Trevor's fingers on the keyboard, Samuel understood with a secret embarrassment that he loved his brother.

One afternoon, their mother banned Trevor from the computer for three hours and told them both to go outside. Under a tree in the orchard, Samuel sat cross-legged while Trevor lay closer to the trunk in deeper shade, his eyes closed, trying, as he'd told Samuel, to retain in his mind the next line of his program.

Samuel watched huge clouds float on the horizon, taller than churches, vacant palaces in the sky.

"Trev?" he said. "You know that teacher of mine that died last year?"

"Hmmm." An American baseball cap shaded his brother's face; he wore trousers and long sleeves, determined that if he had to be outside he would at least prevent himself from getting a tan.

"When he died?" Samuel said. "I knew. Right when it happened."

"Huh-uh."

"But it was before anyone else. We hadn't been told. The school didn't even know. Not till the next day."

"Hmmm," Trevor said. "Maybe you dreamt it. Like Dad and that cousin of his."

"I wasn't dreaming, Trev, I was playing football . . . What about Dad's cousin?"

Trevor pulled tufts of grass from the orchard floor and threw them down over his feet. "We were on holiday up at the Morlands'. You were still a diaper-ridden little rodent, shitting huge volumes of refuse."

"Come on, Trevor."

"Don't deny it. Anyway, it was when those fat Morlands used to give us that bit at the back with the door between where we slept and Mum and Dad's room. Dad had this dream his cousin William had died. I woke up and he was sitting at the edge of the bed, speaking with this funny little quiet voice, saying it was sad William died, going on about how the two of them used to play in the back of Granddad's rope factory. Creepy, really. Then he got up and went back in the other room. *Mum* tried telling me the phone call had come the day before, that they just hadn't told me yet, but I knew he hadn't been on the phone, and I saw him talking on the cordless the next morning out in the garden before breakfast, looking all worried.

"Anyway, we left so they could go to the funeral. I'm probably not supposed to tell you. They give you flack about your whatsit with that teacher last year?"

"Dad swallowed."

"Typical. He needs to develop a new subroutine for anger, that one's dated."

"We're going back to the Wests' for holiday, aren't we?"

"Yes. Again. Same thing three summers running. *Oh, but you like boats, Trevor, and don't tell me you and Peter don't have enormous fun, because you do,"* Trevor said, imitating their mother's matter-of-fact reporting of their inner lives. "Peter West is a rugby-crazed Nazi. He should be taken out and shot."

Samuel waited but Trevor said nothing about Penelope, the sister. Last time they'd gone up, it seemed like Trevor disliked her the way he did with girls he liked.

Samuel himself hated going to Wales. He had to sleep in what seemed more like the cabin of a ship than a bedroom, under a duvet that smelled of seaweed. The Wests' kids were both around Trevor's age; they treated Samuel like a neighbor's dog their parents had sworn them to mind.

"Why do you think Mum and Dad tried hiding it from you like that?" Samuel asked.

"Dad having dreamt it first, you mean?"

"Yeah."

"I don't know, Sam." Patches of bare earth were left where he'd torn up the roots of the grass. "Who knows?" He looked up with a crazed smile. "Maybe you should try bending spoons. I bet you'd get on TV for that." He chuckled, rolling his head back onto the grass. Samuel grabbed his foot and started pulling him across the ground. He kicked back and shouted that Samuel was nothing but a child and then Samuel let go and they wandered into the barn looking about for something to do.

A FEW DAYS later, sitting in the car on the motorway north, Samuel studied the back of his father's head, his shoulder, the thick branch of his upper arm, the dark-haired forearm, his hand gripping the knob of the gearshift. The tired look on his face when he came through the back door from work, the distracted way he ate his dinner, the blur of weekend afternoons when he napped on the front hall couch, all this disappeared when he got behind the wheel of the car. He spoke more, seemed alive in a different way. Samuel thought of this as his father's real self that for some reason only appeared in between places.

Whenever he got picked up from school at the end of a term and they reached the head of the valley—just the two of them—his father would press the car up to ninety miles an hour on the straight country lane and then cut the engine as they swooped onto the downhill. They'd plummet faster and faster, fields whizzing by, the car freewheeling, slowly losing speed as they glided along the valley floor, until eventually they crept at fifteen, ten, five miles an hour, engine still off, seeing how far they could get on initial speed plus gravity: to the Southers' farm or the pub or one time all the way to the foot of the humpback bridge. In the car his father seemed like a magician, in control of everything. Not a man in the middle of the night speaking in a quiet voice of dreams.

They arrived at the Wests' as darkness fell and ate their dinner on their laps in the living room. The house was modern, built onto a cliff on the isle of Anglesey just across the Menai Strait from north Wales. A summer home made for boating, a dock down below. One wall of the living room was glass and through it you could see the lights of houses on the far shore and the lights of a yacht traveling back against the channel's current, returning from a day at sea.

PETER TOOK TREVOR and Samuel out in the canoe the next morning. He was a year younger than Trevor, co-captain of his rugby team. He had a helmet of thick blond hair, a wide neck, and he didn't wear any socks with his trainers.

"Faster!" he called over his shoulder as Trevor and Samuel paddled furiously on the right side of the canoe, their two strokes trying to balance the force of Peter's one to keep the boat on course for the beach out where the strait opened onto the sea. The three of them were racing ahead of Penelope and the adults, who followed behind in a rowboat and a little Sunfish, laden with provisions for lunch and umbrellas for the sun.

Each time Trevor leaned forward to pull his paddle through the water, Samuel could see the muscles in his brother's neck straining. He was thin and had never been particularly strong.

"Move it along, you two," Peter yelled, and Trevor's face went red with exertion.

When the others arrived, towels were handed out and the volleyball net set up. Penelope lay in the sun reading a book. She was two years older than her brother and quieter. The only sport she ever spoke of was sailing, which she did with her father. While the rest of them played volleyball, Trevor and Samuel sat next to her, under the shade of a nearby umbrella, Trevor in his long sleeves.

"What are you reading?" he asked.

"Camus," she said. Her hair was very short and seemed unnaturally pale, a nameless shade between blond and white. There was something very adult about her hair.

"What's the book about?"

"A plague."

"Cool," Trevor said, nodding.

Samuel dug a large hole in the sand in front of him. He felt certain their conversation had something to do with sex.

"You still live in Devon, right?" his brother asked.

"Yeah, it's awful. The point of life in a place so small escapes me."

Trevor seemed to have no reply to this but started talking instead about a software application he had in development that charted people's moods over time. For a year you entered data on your mental state along with thirty variables of diet, weather, geographical location, et cetera, and then the program used the data to predict your mood on future days. When it was done he would try to get the Weather Channel's Web site to offer a link to the download.

"Right," Penelope said, returning to her book.

"Do you ever go to parties?" Trevor asked.

Samuel imagined disappearing into the hole he'd dug in front of him.

"Sometimes," she replied, not looking up from the page. Then Mr. West came by and said it was time for lunch.

That evening a band played at the pub in the village. You had to be fifteen to go, so Samuel stayed behind while the others went. They didn't get back until late, and Peter and Trevor woke him, turning on the light and making noise. They smelled of smoke and beer. Peter got straight into bed and rolled onto his side. Trevor just sat there for a long time on the edge of his bed, staring about.

"Turn the light out, would you?" Peter said. "And while you're at it, stop gawking at my sister."

Trevor made no motion for the lamp. He sat with his elbows on his knees, his chin resting in his hands. With a disgusted huff, Peter got out of bed and switched off the light, leaving Trevor sitting in the dark. Samuel tried to close his eyes and go back to sleep but he couldn't. He lay on his side looking at his brother's outline against the barely visible square of the room's only window. He couldn't think of anything to say. Eventually, Trevor climbed under the sheets, and Samuel kept listening until his breathing went quiet.

IN THE MIDDLE of their second week, the two families took a long hike up Mount Snowdon. The day was hot, the air thin and dry. It was nearly six by the time they returned to the cars. Samuel rode in the back seat with his brother, drifting into sleep along the way. Something heavy was pressing against the side of his head. He saw Giles kicking a football up against a copper beech tree. From all around, in the air, down through the earth, all through his body, Samuel felt the crumpled pity he'd felt that evening on the lawn, but now it was as if Jevins were still alive, were only about to die, as they stood there doing nothing, Giles smiling. But then Jevins was under the white sheet, he was dead, and the pity, that pressure in Samuel's head, became stronger, thick as water all round him. He saw a triangle of sunlight on the water's surface, blackness either side. Trevor was there. The light was blinding him. Samuel heard his brother yell. He stood on the deck of the Wests' house, roofed now in glass. Somewhere behind him a boat's hull shattered. Beneath the glass roof it was no longer the deck, but Trevor's room, clothes tidied into drawers, books piled neatly on the floor by the hard drive, dust on the stacks of twelve-inch singles, a weeping coming from under his mother's door. He saw his father tied to a chair and gagged.

". . . blubbering like a fat infant," he heard, waking to find himself with his face pressed against his brother's shoulder, mouth half open against his shirt, his own body hot with sweat. His mother looked back over her shoulder and smiled. "Having a sleep, are you?"

He turned to the window and saw that they were rising onto the bridge, the sun-dappled waters of the strait running beneath them.

All through supper, his mind remained captive to the dream. The sights and sounds of people at the table reached him from the distance he'd experienced for the first time at school that morning in the dining hall. When coffee and pudding came round, Samuel's father said he was going to fetch a map from the car. Samuel asked to be excused and followed him out the back door into the drive.

"Not having cake?" he said when he turned the corner round the Peugeot and noticed Samuel standing there. He'd spent most of the holiday chatting with Mr. West, napping in the afternoons, encouraging his sons to take up Peter's offers of pickup rugby with his friends.

"Dad?"

"Yes?"

"You know how Mrs. West said Penelope should take Trevor out for a sail?"

"Did she? Right. What about it?"

His father had his hand on the door of the car but hadn't opened it yet.

"You can't let them."

"How do you mean?"

Samuel felt his face go red in the darkness.

"What are you talking about?" his father said.

Clutching his hands into fists, Samuel said, "It's like you and cousin William."

His father stood very still for a moment. Then he walked quickly round the car, coming to stand directly in front of Samuel. He was tall and Samuel only came up to his chest. He wore one of the same blue Oxford shirts he wore each day to work, only rolled at the sleeves and without a tie.

"Now you listen to me," he said in a tone so severe it frightened Samuel. "I suppose it's your brother who saw fit to tell you some story about me and William. It is not true. Do you understand me?"

Samuel could hear the roar and toss of waves against the rocks. Above the line of trees, stars were visible.

"I asked you a question, young man."

"You never believed me when I told you about Mr. Jevins," Samuel said, thankful it was dark enough that his father couldn't see the water welling in his eyes.

"So that's what this is about."

"No!" Samuel said through gritted teeth. "You can't let them go sailing."

His father's hands gripped Samuel's shoulders, his fingers digging into his flesh to the point of pain.

"I'm going to say this once," he said, "so you had better listen. You're twelve years old and you have a lot of ideas in your head, but nothing will wreck you quicker than if you let yourself confuse what's real and what isn't, you hear me? I don't know what it is you're dreaming, or what you dreamt about that teacher, but that's all it is—dreams. Your life's got nothing to do with those shadows, nothing at all.

"If Penelope and Trevor want to go sailing, that's exactly what they'll do. And I don't want to hear you've gone frightening your mother or brother about this nonsense, you understand? You're a perfectly normal boy. Everyone has nightmares. They're tough sometimes. You wake up and you get on with things. That's just how it is. Now you go on into the house and forget about this. Go on." He turned Samuel around and aimed him at the back door.

THEY RETURNED FROM the beach earlier than usual the next day, in the middle of the afternoon, people scattering into various parts of the house to shower or nap. Samuel wandered out onto the deck and found his mother reclining in a chair reading her book. The sun had gone in behind some clouds. She looked up from the page and smiled.

"It's not so bad here, is it?" she said.

Samuel shrugged.

His mother gazed out over the water. "You looking forward to being a prefect next term? You know your father was quite proud when he heard that."

"It'll be all right, I guess."

"Well, I think it's quite something." She turned to admire him. "Aren't you going sailing?"

"Mr. West said he'd had it for the day."

"No, Penelope's taking the boat out, she and Trevor are going. You could probably tag along if you wanted."

He felt a tingling in his hands, the air suddenly live with current. He'd tried to forget his dream as his father had told him to. But he felt sick to his stomach with the memory of it now, and it didn't matter what his father thought.

"You can't let them," he said, nearly whispering.

"What are you talking about?"

"Mum. You have to listen. Trevor, he's going to die out there. You can't let them."

His mother leaned sharply forward, the muscles of her jaw tightening. "How dare you say that," she said. "How dare you say your own brother is going to die. You should be ashamed! What's the matter with you?"

"I know about cousin William, Mum—Trev told me—and you can believe whatever you want about Mr. Jevins, but I *knew,* I fucking *knew—"*

"Samuel!"

"—and yesterday in the car, I dreamt, I did, I dreamt he was dead and there was a sailboat, and I heard him yell. *God,* Mum, why won't you believe me!"

His words seemed to push her back into her chair.

"You dreamt it?" she asked, her tone suddenly flat.

"What's going on here?" Samuel heard his father ask. He

turned to see him standing on the deck behind them. "What's that you just said to your mother?"

"Roger—"

"No, Elizabeth. I will not indulge this. This family is not going to be turned into a madhouse because of some bloody coincidence that happened ten years ago. It's ridiculous. And you, Sam. I thought I'd made myself clear."

His father grabbed him by the arm and pulled him through the kitchen, past Peter, who looked up in surprise from his plate of biscuits, and past Mrs. West in the hall, down the stairs to the boys' room. He sat Samuel down on the bed.

"Now you're going to spend the rest of the day in here, you understand? And you have a good long think about what you've just done—scaring your own mother." His voice was so laden with derision, Samuel thought he might spit on him. But he turned instead and walked out of the room, slamming the door behind him.

Minutes passed. Samuel heard splashing; Penelope called something up to her parents; water sloshed under the dock. He felt as though his mind's eye were being dragged through the wall to watch his brother step onto the boat. A dead, rattling sound filled the air of the room. He couldn't bear it. He hurried to the window, cranked it open as far as it would go, and started yelling, he barely knew what, words coming too quickly, in a jumble. "Stay!" They had to stay here. "Trevor!"

In a moment the door opened behind him, and then his

father had him up against one of the bunk beds. He slapped Samuel hard across the face, bouncing his head off the wood of the bed frame. Then he slapped him again, yelling words Samuel couldn't make out. When his shouting stopped, he turned and left the room.

Later, a few minutes perhaps, a key turned in the knob, locking the door from the outside.

Samuel's body was numb. He sat cross-legged on the floor, holding his head in his hands, the rattling sound still there in his ears. He saw spots darkening brown on his khaki shorts and realized tears were dripping from his cheeks. He wiped them away and stared at the knitted rows of blue carpet dissolving into infinite pattern.

He heard rope chafing on the cleats of the Sunfish, the halyard snapping against the mast. He felt very tired, as if he'd been running through the woods at school for hours and hours, all the coming pain of his brother's death arriving in a wave too strong to survive awake. Trevor. Who had been with him in those spare hours in the house, whose room and company he longed for. His brother who had never made friends of his own, who seemed forever lonely.

It will drive them crazy, he thought, this pain. What Samuel had said, what he knew. There was nowhere for it to go. It would lay his parents' world to ruin. He'd live with his mother somewhere; his father wouldn't be able to bear him. He remembered standing in the main hall with Mr. Kinnet, trying to convince himself it wasn't true about Jevins. He tried with his whole spirit to go back there now, to the place where he could believe it was a stupid dream, that his mind was being squeezed in the fist of some evil pretender. He prayed like they did in chapel, *Give us this day our daily bread and forgive us our trespasses . . .*

The sail flapped in the breeze.

"Ready?" Trevor called.

The window faced east down the strait. Standing by it, Samuel couldn't see the boat. Or the sun emerging from behind the bank of cloud. Only the rays of light striking the bridge's red arch, shining on the water.

"Careful now, you two," he heard his mother call from the deck, the desperation she tried to hide within the rise of her voice not hidden from Samuel.

Then no more sounds. He turned from the window heavy lidded, his body lowering itself down onto the bed. He laid his head on the pillow and sleep dragged him under.

SAMUEL WOKE TO the feeling of a hand against his cheek. His mother was sitting by him on the edge of the bed.

"You should come up for supper," she said. "There's kedgeree and I saved you some lemonade."

He clutched her arm.

"They're fine, Sam, they're fine. They were only gone a little while, they're up there now finishing their dinner. Everything's fine." She ran her hand through his damp hair, a frail look of relief still hovering in the creases of her face.

"He was too hard today, your father, he wasn't fair." Her fingers rubbed his scalp. She looked as though she might cry, but she didn't.

"There are things you don't know, Sam, things that make it hard for him." She paused and looked down at the floor.

Samuel held his mother's hand, muscles he never knew he had letting go with relief. To be here, his mother's pulse against his fingers, her face above him, the most familiar thing in the world, listening to her voice, knowing Trevor was upstairs, the house safely around them. He needed nothing more.

"This business your brother told you about—your father's dream . . . Well, it's true he had that dream. And that they didn't call until the next day, but there's a good reason for that. He'd seen William just the week before down at the hospital in Southampton, and they knew he wasn't doing well so it makes sense he would have a dream about it, because of his health, his cousin's health."

She glanced up at Samuel and then away again, out the window. "Your father gets upset when he hears you talking about knowing these things, or dreaming; he gets worried, because he loves you and he doesn't want you to get confused. It's important you don't get confused. There are coincidences, but it doesn't mean the world doesn't make sense. You can understand that, can't you?"

Samuel sat up and hugged his mother.

"Darling," she said, "if you're having nightmares, if they're bad, we can find someone, someone you can talk with." He closed his eyes and pressed his face against her shoulder.

Upstairs, Peter and Penelope and Trevor all looked at him with a strange curiosity, as if he'd just returned from hospital and they were wondering if he was better. He had after all, he thought to himself, yelled some pretty weird stuff out the window for no reason they could tell. Their caution lasted only briefly. He sat at the table eating his kedgeree and drinking his lemonade. Penelope and Trevor seemed to be getting along a bit now. They played a game of racing demon on the table beside him as he ate his cake.

His father and Mr. West had gone down to the pub. Though he'd slept most of the afternoon, he felt tired enough to go to bed after they all watched a video. His mother gave him another hug in the hallway, just outside their bedroom. Trevor came over and joined them.

"Went a bit weird there, hey, Sammy?"

"Yeah," Samuel said, holding back tears at the feeling of his brother's arms around him.

IT WAS IN the middle of a light shower the following afternoon that the two of them set off in the car to get vegetables and bread from the village. According to Penelope, who was escorted back to the house only a little while later unharmed, the sun appeared just as the rain ended, a triangle of light glistening on the black pavement, and onto the windshield, causing Trevor to slant into the right lane. The car ripped into the side of the oncoming van before hitting the swerving trailer, the impact smashing the hull of a white sailboat in tow.

Samuel sat on the back steps, waiting for his parents to return from the hospital. When they pulled up to the house, hours later, they saw him there. They didn't get out of the car right away. The eyes of their pale, haggard faces stared at him through the windshield. From the kitchen he could hear a radio playing, the murmur of singing voices.

A broken spirit. That's what Jevins said God wanted. A broken and contrite heart. Was this the God of the vast landscape, out where Samuel knew now he would spend the rest of his days? The quiet place, beyond the walls of the crowded dwelling.

A broken spirit. Would that be enough?

MY FATHER'S BUSINESS

THE COMMUTER TRAIN is barely out of South Station when it comes slowly to a halt. The lights go out, the hum of the air conditioner ceases. It's a midmorning in June and the railcar is three-quarters empty. Daniel sits toward the back, by a window, the envelope still sealed on his lap.

In the sudden absence of noise, he can hear the sounds of his fellow passengers: a newspaper being folded, a boy two rows up whispering to his father, a cough, and a yawn. Weak morning light, filtered through an overcast sky, hangs in the rail yard, scarcely making it through the train's tinted windows.

He sips the last of his ginger ale and watches a blue Conrail engine creep along the tracks in front of the huge Gillette sign. A work crew in orange vests idles by a switch in the rail, waiting for the engine to pass. Above them, gulls circle the pylons.

In this unexpected quiet, Daniel realizes there is part of him that doesn't want to open the file, doesn't want to read the interviews or what the doctors have to say about them. Their words won't change anything. But then he doesn't want to be afraid of himself either.

It wasn't easy getting the records. Gollinger, his psychiatrist, didn't want him to see the correspondence. But it was in the file, Daniel had a right to it. And another part of him is glad that somewhere in the confusion his life has become, he found the energy and organizational wherewithal to obtain them. Perhaps it will help him to remember, help him see things clearly.

Through his feet, he feels a vibration accompanied by a clicking sound, and then the hiss of the brakes releasing. The train lurches forward, lights flicker on, the air hums again. At the end of the line is the town Daniel grew up in, a place he hasn't been in years.

He undoes the metal clasp and with his forefinger breaks the seal. Inside is a packet of paper, half an inch thick. He flips through it and, putting aside the test results and Gollinger's scribbled notes, begins to read.

WINSTON P. GOLLINGER, M.D.
231 PINE STREET
BROOKLINE, MASSACHUSETTS 02346

November 15, 1997

Dr. Anthony Houston
McLean's Hospital
115 Mill Street
Belmont, MA 02478

Dear Tony,

Thank you for your letter of November 10 concerning Daniel Markham. The tapes he's mentioned to you are not a fabrication. He recorded several of them over the last six months. On his final visit to my office he asked that I take them for safekeeping. I've had my secretary type out a transcript, which is enclosed with this letter.

Daniel Markham came to me eighteen months ago suffering from alternating states of mania and depression. He was twenty-four, his parents were divorced, he was unemployed, single, and occasionally using narcotic painkillers, which he had a prescription for due to a long-standing back condition. Based on family history, notably a father with active bipolar disorder and Daniel's own reports of labile mood states, a diagnosis of bipolar (I) wasn't difficult to make. I began aggressive drug treatment and weekly consultations. Multiple drug regimens failed to produce significant changes in Daniel's disease.

The tapes themselves center on what Daniel described as his "research." Eight months ago he began talking about what he called "an anecdotal sociology of the philosophical urge in young men." Coming as it did, as one in a series of manic projects and ideas, I took no particular note of it, other than the obvious connection with Daniel's father, who, when he was younger, had earned a Ph.D. in philosophy and had been forced to leave his teaching position due to a depressive episode. Over the months, however, Daniel demonstrated what was, for him, an unusual consistency of interest in the project.

As you may have discovered for yourself by now, Daniel is often a charming person to be with, and it was hard to watch his situation decline. Hopefully under your care, in an inpatient setting, he will stabilize. Don't hesitate to call if you have further questions.

Sincerely,
Winston P. Gollinger, M.D.

TRANSCRIPT OF TAPES RECORDED BY DANIEL MARKHAM, MARCH 15–AUGUST 12, 1997

1. Interview with Daniel Markham's father, Charles Markham

—Date is March 15th, ides of March . . . first entry on the Dictaphone . . . got it tied around my neck here . . .

so . . . Dad's here, he's talking about—Dad?—I'm putting this on the research, okay?

—Which, given the rates in the bond market at the moment, is just absurd and I told him that, Danny, six and a quarter, maybe six and a half, and we could float the whole offering, the street would soak the paper up in a minute, and your sister and you could get a house, a boat . . .

—Is that Dr. Fenn still there at the clinic, Dad?

—Yeah, he's there, but I—if they'd just take a promissory note and once I get into the currency markets it's child's play—cross market arbitrage—the yen and the ruble, the lira and the pound, an eighth of a cent here, a twentieth there, a big enough stake, and I mean they understand this down at the Fed, they know that I'd be a stabilizing force in the market, and with all the bad paper on the street—

—Do you see him much?

—Who?

—Dr. Fenn.

—He has dogs.

—In his office?

—Why are you in bed, Danny?

—I told you, Dad. My back. It's killing me, it's been killing me for months.

—He keeps them in a cement yard behind the clinic—three schnauzers and a Great Dane—they beshit themselves and I don't like doctors who keep animals in that condition. Besides, he's a behaviorist.

—But you have appointments with him, right? Sometimes?

—I don't think he's ever published an article in his life and when I go in there with a new study from *Science* or *New England Journal of Medicine* he gets very defensive. I always prefer doctors who publish . . . but anyway, there's an underlying crisis at Treasury. Bond issues have been selling poorly and with the advance of the Euro there could be a flight from the dollar, which at the moment is the only benchmark currency we have, but that might change and if I can get in there, get in there with a stake—

—Help me for a second, Dad.

—What?

—The pills on the bureau.

—Okay, okay. But do you hear what I'm saying? Everything could change, I could buy the old house back and that ugly pine hedge could be dug up and replaced with a Japanese maple tree like the one your mother planted, the smooth bark—

—Dad.

—Those small shiny leaves almost like the petals of a flower—

—The water glass—

—Spread like a fine carpet on the lawn, if I could just get in there with a stake—do you have paper somewhere, I have to write a letter to my bank and we can get it messengered downtown.

—Help me, please. Turn this off, here around my neck . . .

—Why are you wincing, Danny?

—Please.

—You must have paper somewhere.

2. *Interview with Daniel Markham's roommate, Al Turpin*

—April 4th, we've got my roommate, Al, here. Al? Do you want to say something?

—Is this like a time capsule?

—I told you, it's the start of the research. It's a record, some confirmation that something's happening.

—Right, well, I guess I feel like a lot is happening. I mean the whole idea of selling those old futons to help with the rent. I think that's all gone really well. It's very shrewd.

—All right, Al, but we're doing the anecdotal sociology now, so let's just move on. All right?

—Sure.

—Okay . . . we're going to begin here with my friend Al Turpin, who's twenty-six, an office temp, and he's agreed to talk to us about his interest in philosophy . . . we're just starting by asking people how it began.

—Well, the first thing I remember is my sister coming home from college and saying to me: "Scratch an altruist and watch a hypocrite bleed." We were sitting out by the lake, and I felt this sudden flutter of excitement in my chest. The idea seemed so powerful, that I could know such a thing. Now I mostly just read. Like after work, I'll come home and pick up whatever I'm working my way through, Leibniz or Hegel or whatever, and I'll read a few pages, take some notes, just try to understand what they're saying. It's kind of like reading a big, very long story, starts with Zeno and those guys and then there are all these installments, all these episodes, and you don't read it in order, you just get this idea of the overall structure of the story, the plot I guess, and you fill in the parts you don't have. Some of it's really boring. Like Spinoza. But you got to do it. I don't know why really. You just have to.

—Can you describe reading the books, Al, the actual experience?

—That's hard. I'd say the main thing is the sense of order. The sense that even if you can't perceive the whole architecture of the argument at any given point, you know there is an architecture, that you're in this man's hands in a way, being carried along toward the completion of a vision, something he's seen and is revealing to you slowly. There's a tremendous comfort in that kind of order, even if you can't see it . . . By the way, did that Dutch guy who called about a futon say when he was coming?

3. Interview with Daniel Markham's friend, Kyle Johnson

—Yeah, just sit there, that's fine. Okay, okay, we have Kyle here, a good friend of mine from Bradford High, and he's going to talk to us, okay, okay, so tell us how the whole philosophy thing got started for you.

—Dan?

—Yeah?

—Are you all right?

—Me? Sure, sure. Fire away. You want some coffee? Al, get him some coffee.

—You look a little harried.

—I'm fine, really. So how did it start?

—Dan. I know it hasn't been easy lately. I heard about your dad going back in the hospital. I remember all that stuff when we were kids. To tell you the truth I haven't been so great myself. But I'm saying if you ever need a place to stay or anything.

—That's very, very, very kind of you, Kyle. Now about philosophy.

—Have you been seeing your doctor?

—Whose fucking inquisition is this anyway?

—Okay, Dan, okay.

—All right, then. Philosophy.

—Well, I guess it began in the barn.

—The barn, okay, tell us about the barn.

—There was a room in the barn. A room I used to play in. No. Wait. I have to go back. I have to tell you about the newspaper.

—Okay, the newspaper, tell us about the newspaper.

—When I was ten I started a newspaper. It was called the *Hammurabi Gazette*.

—After the famous legal code.

—No. My cat was named Hammurabi. The paper was devoted to coverage of his life.

—You never told me you had a cat.

—Yeah, I had one.

—Go on.

—There were feature articles about Hammurabi and his daily life. Pictures too. My brother wrote a monthly crossword made up of the nicknames we had for Hamm. There was a sports page as well. We set up a miniature Olympiad for him and photographed him knocking over little hurdles. My father photocopied the paper at his office. Relatives in Canada subscribed to it.

—So you got into philosophy from a publishing angle?

—No, wait, you have to listen.

—Okay, okay.

—In the barn there was a room. No, Al, I said I don't take milk. The barn was old. It was rotting. My parents didn't like me to play there, but I did. In the floor of the room there was a small trapdoor that opened onto the stables. They used to throw the hay down through it. I was angry at Billy Hallihan. He had deflated the tires of my bicycle the day before at school and laughed as I pumped them up again. I asked him over to play in the barn. I knew he'd come because the barn was cool. The barn was falling apart. Before he came I opened the trapdoor. The door swung downward. I covered the square hole with paper. Old copies of the *Hammurabi Gazette,* stapled together. My plan was that I would stand on the far side of the room. When Billy entered I would say, “Come over here, I have something to show you.” He would walk across the room, step onto the paper, and his leg would go through the hole. My sense was that his entire body would not go through it. That he would just be hurt and embarrassed. I put the paper over the hole and went back outside to ride my bike until he arrived. When I saw him coming across the yard, I hurried back into the barn. The paper was gone. I walked up to the hole. I looked down. In the stable below there was an old rusting sit-down lawn mower that my brother and I had taken half to pieces. I had removed the plastic knob from the gearshift. That’s where Hammurabi had landed. On the spike of that metal stick that I had uncovered, falling through the trap I had laid with my paper devoted to him. Hamm had carried a copy of the *Gazette* down with him, and it too was impaled.

—Jesus Christ.

—Yes. The image is not so different. He died for my sins.

—You never told me this, Kyle. So this eventually led to what?

—Kant. Rawls. Moral theory of one kind or another.

—And you studied that in college.

—Yeah.

—And now you work at the bakery, right?

—No, I left there a couple weeks ago. Somebody stole a bread slicer, they pegged it on me.

—So what are you doing?

—I work at a cemetery. I'm a groundsman, I prepare the graves.

—Get outta here! You're a grave digger!

—They don't call them that anymore. Just like they don't call bank tellers bank tellers. But yeah, that's what I am.

—Where?

—Out in Bradford, that little cemetery behind Saint Mary's.

—You're kidding me! Is this a temporary thing?

—I don't know. I don't know how I would know. The future is a mystery to me.

—I'm so glad you came, Kyle, I'm in the process of developing this new way to map human experience, the research here is part of it, interviewing people. I want to figure out the relationship between the desire for theoretical knowledge and certain kinds of despair. This cat stuff is very interesting in that regard.

—Is your dad better since he got out?

—Wonderful. Just wonderful.

—I never had the same energy you did, Dan.

—Don't be silly, don't be silly, this is all extremely interesting.

—It's strange being out in Bradford again. Something peaceful about it, though. You could come out and visit me sometime, if you needed somewhere to go.

—Sure, sure. Al, what are you doing?

—Shhhh. Listen. There's someone at the door.

—Who is it, Al?

—I don't know. I think it's the super.

4. Interview with Wendell Lippman

—Daniel Markham conducting interview number three, June 16th, 1997, Anecdotal Sociology of the Philosophical Urge in Young Men, funding pending at the National Endowment for the Humanities, the National Center for Mental Health, Centers for Disease Control, United States Departments of the Interior, Health and Human Services, and Education. Proceeding number 3B1997. Subject, Wendell O. Lippman, Caucasian male, age twenty-one, resident of Jamaica Plain, Boston. First question. Mr. Lippman, could you state your full name for the record?

—Wendell Oliver Lippman.

—Thank you. Now, Mr. Lippman, you have come here to

participate in some groundbreaking research. What you say here today could alter the daily lives of millions of your fellow citizens. I don't want to sound overly serious, but you need to understand you are sitting now at a kind of apex, an unparalleled position of influence, one you may never again attain in your life, a chance to shape the future of a nation by opening a window into the souls of its young men. Do you feel ready for this responsibility?

—I guess so. I mean, I just met Al the other day, at the park.

—Mr. Lippman, you must understand. In this instance Mr. Turpin is only a conduit through whom you have come to me. Your association with him is an empirical necessity but otherwise entirely irrelevant. This study is interested in you qua you, not you qua friend of Al. Is that clear?

—What does "qua" mean?

—Mr. Lippman, is it your impression that *I* am conducting this interview, or is it rather your impression that *you* are conducting this interview?

—You, I guess.

—That is correct, Mr. Lippman, that is correct.

—Look, man, I mean, Al just said I should come over sometime 'cause, you know, we could talk about God and stuff like that, which is cool and all, but . . . I was just coming by to pick up some weed.

—For the record, I am now granting myself permission to treat the subject as hostile.

—What?

—State the titles and authors of the books you have read in the last five years.

—All of them?

—Yes, Mr. Lippman, all of them.

—You're fucking intense.

—Are we done now with the editorial comment?

—Yeah.

—Good. So you've read what, exactly?

—Well, I checked this thing out on the Gulf War, about how, like, there was all this information about it, but not really any analysis, and that was sort of a new thing.

—Could you state for the record your level of education?

—I go to college.

—Right. Passing on the book question for now, perhaps you could tell us something about your interest in philosophy and how it began. You do have an interest in philosophy, correct?

—Sure.

—All right. Tell us how it got started.

—Well, the first time I got high—

5. Interview with Carl de Hooten

—We're talking here this afternoon with Carl de Hooten . . . who is twenty-seven years old and a resident of western Somerville. Mr. de Hooten—

—Carl's fine.

—All right. Carl is a—how did you describe it?

—A freelance graduate student.

—A freelance grad student. Meaning?

—I'm affiliated with a number of departments.

—He is a graduate of SUNY Oswego, where he studied philosophy. So, Carl, tell us something about your initial interest in the field.

—Where I lived as a child, a neighboring girl began a lemonade stand, her plan being to sell to passersby. My mother decided that I ought to participate in this venture, a sentiment which I later concluded derived from her conviction that I did not leave the house frequently enough. I fought her suggestion tooth and nail, having no interest in hawking some sugar drink to the locals. My mother persisted, however, going as far as to contact the girl's parents and negotiate my inclusion. I was told to go and sit by the girl at the table—to go and have fun. It was through the experience of sitting beside this girl—Verena was her name—that I became interested in artificial intelligence. In front of the table, Verena had hung a sign which announced the price of a lemonade at twenty cents. The interesting thing, however, was that despite the sign she charged different customers different prices. If her friend Judy came by, for instance, she was invariably allowed to pay only a nickel. Boys were generally charged five cents over—a full quarter—on the claim that the sign referred only to the price of the lemonade, and not the cost of the cup. When cars slowed to make a purchase, she'd slap me across the shoulders and insist I kneel down in front of the table, thus obscuring the sign and allowing her to bilk the strangers for fifty cents or even a dollar. When I said I thought this was unfair, she took my face in her hands and yelled at me, saying, "You are only here because my mother says you have to be." Around this same time I had been taking apart a calculator my father had given me, checking out the circuits, looking through a magnifying glass at the chip, imagining all those microscopic chambers inside, how every calculation was broken down into its binary constituents. I was watching Verena one afternoon, watching the expression on her face as three older girls approached from up the road. I could see her trying to decide what to charge, and it struck me that if one knew enough about her brain, if one could get down into the synapse, down into the interstitial fluid, to the binary code, well, then she'd be predictable, even reproducible, and all the apparent capriciousness, all the malleability would succumb to an algorithm, a chip on a motherboard. That's more or less how it got started.

—Interesting . . .

—I've been pretty heavily into artificial intelligence ever since: neural nets, cognitive modeling.

—Ask him if he's ever had a girlfriend.

—Al! I apologize, my roommate's—

—That's all right, I can answer if you like. The fact is I haven't had a girlfriend.

—Does this bother you?

—It occasionally bothers me intensely and I feel like an outcast, and then for long stretches I don't even notice. I must say, though, coming here is comforting.

—Why's that?

—It makes me feel like a stable person, in control of my life.

—Coming here does?

—Yeah, I mean look at you guys. You're living in these rooms so full of books you can barely move, your roommate's lying on his stomach on the floor, he's been there for an hour—

—He's got gastrointestinal problems—

—And you're sitting there with a bag of ice on your back and a Dictaphone asking these questions . . . and this is all somehow part of you selling me a futon? This isn't normal, you know. There's nothing normal about it.

6. Interview with Charles Markham

—Okay, Dad, it's on . . . Are you going to say something?

—Day's almost over.

—I can turn on a light if you want.

—It's all right . . . What are we supposed to talk about?

—I told you, I'm doing this research, about how the interest in philosophy begins, what it leads to . . .

—You don't want to interview me.

—I do.

—Danny, it's all over now. Why do you want to drag it up? They fired me, that's all.

—It's not about the job. This isn't about academics, I just mean how it got started for you, what it meant to you . . .

—Funny. What it meant to me? I was reading this book the other day. There's this fragment I remember. Went something like, *People whose best hope for a connection to other human beings lay in elaborating for themselves an elegiac mode of relatedness, as if everyone's life were already over.* Seemed accurate to me.

—How do you mean?

—This idea of living your life as an elegy, inoculating yourself against the present. So much easier if you can see people as though they were just characters from a book. You can still spend time with them. But you have nothing to do with their fate. It's all been decided. The present doesn't really matter, it's just the time you happen to be reading about them. Which makes everything easier. Other people's pain, for instance.

—Did this have something to do with what got you started reading?

—The philosophers—they were part of that, keeping things at a remove.

—How?

—They were my friends. Reliable. There to keep me company. You spent time with them, they talked to you. They didn't have crises. They were always ready with a little numbered comment. So ideal that way. No dying bodies to drag around. Like a painting. No changes, no disappointments. Everything already over.

—Did you read when you were in the hospital? Mom said you always had your books.

—What are you talking about?

—The year you were on the ward.

—She told you about that, about me being in there?

—Yeah. She said she used to come and read to you . . . Look at me, Dad . . . Say something.

—Turn that tape thing off, would you? Oh Danny, why are you crying?

—And she said, she said the doctor told her you were sick . . .

—Stop it.

—And that you needed your family . . . Where are you going? Dad. Where are you going?

—I have to go.

—No, Dad, please. I want to talk to you, come on, you said you'd do the interview, please, this is for me—the research—come on, you can't leave now, please . . . What about the day you picked me up from school in your tux—Dad?—with that Lamborghini, and we went to the Harbor and you bought me martinis and dinner and we stayed the night—tell me what it felt like, tell me what you were thinking—

—No, Danny, I have to—

—That week you slept in the garage or the time you made

the sculpture in the living room, come on, I want you to tell me how it all fit in, how the books fit in, the theories, the things you read, Dad!

7. Daniel Markham, self-interview

—Anecdotal Sociology interview number something, Daniel Markham . . . So, Mr. Markham, could you tell us a little something about yourself? . . . Surely, I was born in Boston, we were all in the hospital there, me, my mom, and my dad too! . . . Your dad? . . . Yes, he too had a room, just over in the next wing . . . You're such a kidder . . . I know, doesn't it just kill you . . . So seriously now, to the topic at hand, why have you laid all your books out on the floor like this, and why have you stacked them in front of the door and why won't you let Al in, and why, Mr. Markham, why are you naked, and why do you lie on top of these books, and do you really have a back condition, or is that just an elaborate somatoform pose, and do you really have an ulcer that won't let you sleep, and do you really spend the day in a ghastly neurasthenic haze, and just what are those things you've started to draw on the wall that look vaguely like the symbols of some primitive religion, and what would Dr. Gollinger think of them, hey? And is it the circles in them that interests you, or the lines that cut across them, like the spike of the gearshift on which that cat landed? . . . All very interesting, yes, I agree, but really you'll have to be more specific. I mean, what exactly is the question? . . . Well, it's your own question, Mr. Markham, don't you remember it? You asked them how their interest in philosophy began, so how did it begin for you? . . . Interesting yes, very interesting, the tears, I think it was the tears, or rather the pages wrinkled with the dried tears, the open book on his desk, my father's of course, and then a paragraph where the paper was wrinkled, raised, you know the way paper gets when it's been wet and then dried, just a few circles here and there, and no water glass in sight, and of course the other minor evidence being that he was weeping on the sofa. Reading those wrinkled paragraphs, looking at the little black words, listening to my father cry, well you see, it was all so fascinating and captivating to me, and I just said, gosh darn it, I'd love a career in this sort of thing . . . There you go again, you crack me up, really this is supposed to be a serious interview . . . Sorry, I know, I know . . . And so what have you learned? . . . Well I'm glad you finally asked me that because you see, that's why I keep the books all over the floor like this, and why I like to lie on top of them, because really then reference becomes much easier, I mean I can just feel the *Symposium* pressing up against my thigh here, but seriously, what I've learned, well there's so much, but let's see, Kant said I'm clearing away knowledge to make room for faith, and Marx said there is only one antidote to mental suffering, and that is physical pain (which seems accurate to me), and Kierkegaard said there are many people who reach their conclusions about life like schoolboys, they cheat their masters by copying the answers from a book, and Vico said the criterion and rule to truth is to have invented the truth, maybe even conducted a few interviews, who knows? And Wittgenstein said ethics and aesthetics are one and the same thing, and he said the solution to the problem of life is seen in the vanishing of the problem, and he said I can only doubt if there is something beyond doubt, and Heidegger said the idea of logic itself disintegrates in the turbulence of a more original questioning, and Fichte said—No, Al, I'm not hungry, I'm doing an interview, I'll be out tomorrow, go out, enjoy yourself, it's a lovely day . . . A warning? . . . Burn it, Al! It's just a collection notice. Just burn it, burn the whole fucking stack, the phone and electric, just burn it in a pyre on the landing and strap that fucking nosy super to it! You can do it, Al, you can do it! . . . You were saying, Mr. Markham . . . Yes, I was saying Fichte said something too, and so did Pascal, and my mother said we all fall apart in little ways, and then there's the passage here, the one I can't stop reading, where is it? Here in the gospel, Luke, Chapter Two. *And it came to pass, that after three days they found him in the temple, sitting in the midst of the doctors, both hearing them, and asking them questions. And all that heard him were astonished at his understanding and answers. And when they saw him, they were amazed: and his mother said unto him, Son, why hast thou thus dealt with us? behold, thy father and I have sought thee sorrowing. And he said unto them, How is it that ye sought me? wist ye not that I must be about my Father's business?* . . . My father's business . . . Open to any page. Here, take a book, Mr. Markham, yes there, that wetted paragraph, read the words.

[end of final tape]

MCLEAN'S HOSPITAL
115 MILL STREET
BELMONT, MA 02478

Office of Dr. Anthony Houston

February 11, 1998

Winston P. Gollinger, M.D.
231 Pine Street
Brookline, Massachusetts 02346

Dear Win,

You inquired about the progress of Daniel Markham. As of a week ago, he is no longer a patient at the hospital, having checked himself out.

He was under my care for three months. After coming off his initial manic high, he was moderately to severely depressed nearly every day of his stay. I tried several drug regimens, some with partial efficacy. If there was any real progress, and I'm not sure there was, it came in our twice-weekly therapy sessions.

Here he exhibited brief periods of animation. Once I'd read the transcript and listened to the tapes I was able to engage him on the topic of philosophy. This seemed to provide some bearing for him. A friend named Kyle Johnson brought him books and this appeared to boost his mood somewhat. The nurses report that on his better days he spent most of his time reading.

Around Christmas, his father made an unfortunate visit to the hospital. He was in a full-blown manic episode, soliciting staff and nurses for investments in an offshore hedge fund. Needless to say, the visit didn't help Daniel, and a week later I increased his dosage of Depakote.

We both know these refractory cases are out there. We did the best we could. Without medication, I'd be surprised if Charles Markham doesn't commit suicide within five years. Daniel's still young, the course of his disease difficult to predict.

If I hear anything further I will contact you. If Daniel reenters treatment with you, please let me know.

Sincerely,
Anthony Houston, M.D.

THE TRAIN CLICKS past the backyards of Bradford. One strewn with children's plastic toys. Another with its ground churned up, ready for the sod of a new lawn. Daniel leans his head against the glass, letting his eyes drop out of focus, the trees becoming a gentle blur. Without looking, he takes the papers from his lap and places them facedown on the seat beside him. Soon the train begins to slow. At Bradford Hills, he watches the father two rows up gather his briefcase under one arm, take his young son by the hand, and walk down the aisle. Emptier still, the train moves on, past the tennis courts and baseball fields where Daniel played as a child, past the supermarket where he bagged groceries after school and the police station where he and his mother used to file the missing persons reports.

Have they picked him up, he wonders, dressed in a swimsuit in a supermarket aisle, pleading with a stranger to read a sheet of paper he clasps in his hands? Or is he at the apartment he mentioned the last time they spoke, some friend Daniel had never heard of, a woman who told fortunes? That he can sit placidly on this train and imagine any of this astonishes Daniel. That in this moment of reprieve he feels neither despair nor exaltation.

Just behind the post office, the train comes to a halt at Bradford Square. He takes up the papers, the envelope, the empty soda can, lifts himself from the seat.

The day has become warm, the dampness of the morning rain lingering in the air. He climbs the staircase into the parking lot and heads across it toward Washington Street. The sidewalks have been redone with brick, and there are new benches and lampposts, all painted the same dark green. There are even more Mercedes and Jaguars than he remembers, even more wealthy young mothers with painted faces and gold jewelry, pushing strollers by restaurants and boutiques. He walks past the library. By the pay phone there is a garbage can, and into it he throws the file and all its contents: the test reports, the duplicate prescriptions, the blood levels, the doctors' notes, the interviews, the predictions of experts.

At the Pond Street intersection, he waits for the walk sign and then crosses. The sun is nearly out, playing faint shadows on the sidewalk, beginning to glisten against the road's wet pavement. The tires of the passing cars make a swishing sound as they go by. A warm breeze drifts over the street and into the budding trees.

Ahead, he sees the sign for Saint Mary's. A path leads up to the church's brick tower and then heads off down the side of the building. He follows the path around to the gate. The cemetery is no more than a couple of acres, crowded with headstones and flowers. At the back, they've cleared a copse of trees to make room for a few more parishioners. He sees the line of Kyle's shoulders hunched over a wheelbarrow, and closing the gate behind him, makes his way over the carefully tended grass.

"Dan," Kyle says, looking up from his work on the grave, "you made it."

For a moment, here, in the calm he knows is only the eye of the storm, in the center of a turbulence that, despite everything anyone has ever written or said, might not mean a thing, he can only stare into his friend's gentle face, and listen, with gratitude, to the sounds of the world around him.

THE VOLUNTEER

I

THE BOY HAS given her hope, a hope Elizabeth never imagined she'd have again. Seven weeks in a row he has come to visit her. An awkward teenager, lonely she suspects, curious in ways that will not help him defeat others in the competition for success. He comes with a pad and pencils and asks her what she would like him to draw. Her walls are decorated with his work: sketches of the woods behind his house, the view from this window, but mostly self-portraits, conventional at the outset by the mirror, growing more expressive as they progress across the wall, his eyes growing small, his forehead larger, the pencil's lead smudged to blur the lines. His visits have given her weeks a purpose. She spends hours imagining their conversation, thinking of questions she wants to ask, and then like a nervous mother forgets them when he arrives.

From her window, Elizabeth watches the day ending out in the harbor. Cloud is filling the sky from the east, tarnishing the blue waves, leaving only a pale strip of light fading across the Atlantic horizon. Soon it will be time to eat. She will walk the tiled corridor, past the rooms of her fellow residents, into the dining hall, where Marsha, the cook, will wave to her, and she will take her seat at the table and consume the starchy food. If there is such a thing as a placid bell, then it is the bell that rings for supper at the Plymouth Brewster Structured Living Facility at five-thirty every day of the year. Hearing its soft chime, Elizabeth turns back into the room, and putting on her cardigan and slippers, commences her daily journey.

Later, on her return, she sees the Primidone tablets waiting in their white paper cup on her bedside table, placed there as always by Judith, the staff nurse. For more than two decades, Elizabeth Maynard has done exactly as she is told and the voice of Hester, which has cost her so much, comes only quietly and intermittently. It is a negative sort of achievement, she thinks, to have spent a life warding something off. These last few weeks, try though she has, there have been moments during Ted's visits when Elizabeth got stuck in the medication's sludge, patches of time slowing to a halt. The boy has reminded her of what there is to miss. She only wants to know him as a person would. In her heart, she can't believe this is too much to ask. It might do her good to have a little break, she muses to herself, placing the tablets at the back of her dresser drawer.

"STOP FUCKING TRYING would you!" his brother yells from downstairs as Ted stands at their mother's bedroom door calling softly, "Are you awake?"

"If you're not in my car in twenty seconds you're walking!" John shouts from the kitchen. Ted tries the handle, but as usual it's locked. He wants to see if she's okay, but there's no time now so he grabs his book bag from his room and skips down the stairs.

In the car, his brother plays *Rage Against the Machine* loud enough to make the seats vibrate. He runs two stop signs and doesn't speak the whole way to school. Finally, in the parking lot, Ted slips on his headset and a British rock star's lilting voice sweeps everything from his mind: *She walks in beauty like the night, ba ba ba ba ba da da,* followed, as he climbs the front steps, by words he can never make out, *Marilyn* something, and then at last, as he turns into the corridor, the part he's been waiting for, *I'm aaaaching to see my heroine, I'm aaaaching to see my heroine,* his head swooning to the rise of the vocal line, a line of bliss, followed by a tap on the shoulder—Mr. Ananian's lips saying, "Turn that thing off."

The stop button clicks in his ears.

"I'm not telling you again."

Twenty-odd students slumped on their tan Formica desks, forty-five minutes of advanced algebra, not a hope of seeing Lauren Jencks. He feels ill.

"Oh my God," he says, working a quizzical expression, "I totally forgot my notebook—I'll be right back," and he turns into the hall, walking quickly away, the door slamming behind him.

"Way to go," Stevie Piper says, giving him a thumbs-up as he darts out of a chemistry class. "You got to come tonight, man—Phoebe Davidson's parents are outta town."

"Sure," Ted says, hurrying down the hall toward the art wing, where Lauren has life drawing. He's nervous already about her spotting him at the door of the classroom, though he knows she knows he's been looking at her for weeks, even months, ever since she arrived at school the beginning of term.

Mrs. Theodopoulos has a photograph of a dog set on an easel at the front of the class and she's using a pointer to direct her students' attention to the dog's ear. The kids, their backs to Ted, smudge charcoal on drawing paper, doing ears. Lauren's in the second row: faded orange cardigan with the pockets stretched open, a bar of sunlight slanting across her back, a patch of her short brown hair shining above her ear, no earring. He loves the fact she doesn't wear rings or necklaces or makeup and how large her eyes are and how she seems about ten years older than he is, as though she's traveled the world five times over and for some mysterious reason, bad karma or whatever, is being made to repeat life in high school. In his room at night, when he demurely puts his image of her aside to jack off to the cruder images on the Net, he thinks she must want to tell someone how that's been, to have to return from such distant places. If on certain rare occasions he does let himself undress her, she's always on top, her back arched, her eyes closed, this look on her face as though she's remembering another time, but then as he's about to come she opens her eyes and leans down and they stare at each other before he rises up to kiss her, exploding.

From where he's standing, hard now thinking about her, he can't see her dog's ear. He leans his head in against the glass, trying to catch a glimpse of the side of her face, her hand, the drawing, leaving out of his field of vision the approaching juggernaut of Mrs. Theodopoulos storming the aisle, ballistic finger outstretched. She is halfway to the door when he sees her, the class turning now to watch, his heart thudding.

Giddy, he dodges and runs.

From the third floor walkway he can see across the courtyard, through the window, over Mrs. Theodopoulos's shoulder, and into the first two rows of the art room. Since Lauren's friends started laughing at the sight of him a few weeks back he's known there is no point in playing it cool. He stares at her without pretense. Bring it on, he thinks, bring on the ridicule, go ahead, call me pathetic and ugly and desperate, snicker at me, roll your eyes, say you'd never touch me in a million years, that you'd all rather sleep with a monkey, go ahead, shout it.

No one seems to be watching him. They scrawl at their

papers, minds still in bed, bodies drowsing through first period.

Then it happens. She looks up over her easel, and squinting, sees him. She smiles. He is sure of it. Lauren Jencks has identified him at thirty yards, and she's smiling—at him or with him, he doesn't dare to guess. He plays it cool, waves casually, starts walking away. It is decided then, he will take his tray to her table today, giggling friends be damned.

He knows he must calm himself before they meet.

In the bathroom stall he tries reading a page on the battle of Shiloh but gives up and hurriedly imagines four blond girls licking his naked body, chiding himself as he goes for his lack of originality, but relieved, when he is done, to breathe deeply for the first time that morning.

ELIZABETH WAKES TO colors more vivid: the Oriental carpet's swirls of burgundy and gold; dawn kindling the sky an immaculate blue. She puts on her bathrobe and moves to her spot by the window. Planes of the rising sun sparkle in the courtyard's frosted grass. It is the washed light of autumn that shone on the lawn of the hospital down on the Connecticut coast, the hospital where Elizabeth stayed a month the year before she and Will were married—this memory arriving now with unaccustomed ease.

He would come down from Cambridge on Sundays in his father's old Lincoln Town Car. They'd take walks on the cliffs overlooking Long Island Sound. He was a bookish man, nervous. Like Elizabeth, he'd grown up in New England in a house of lapsed Episcopalians, raised like her on a liberal conscience, parents sighing resignedly over the *New York Times,* salvation—if there were such a thing—a promise of reform rather than redemption. Together she and Will managed hours of politeness with no mention of Elizabeth's reasons for being in an institution—her little *confusions,* as her parents called them—the occasional trouble remembering where she was, the rarer sense she was being spoken to. Will was completing his doctorate in sociology at Harvard and they spoke of that. They'd met in his discussion section the semester before she'd taken a leave from Radcliffe, a school her parents still hoped back then she might return to.

Toward the end of her stay, Will had an appointment alone with her psychiatrist. Elizabeth behaved badly, listening at the door. "A mild imbalance," the man said. She has never known if he was merely a sexist who thought her hysterical or a kind man who understood what Will meant to her, perhaps even a man who let his kindness supervene his judgment. When Will asked him if they should still get married, the doctor asked if he loved his fiancée. Elizabeth never felt as safe as she did when she heard Will say, "Yes," without stopping to consider. "Then you should marry her," the doctor replied.

After the wedding, they took her parents' summer home in the town next to Plymouth, an old saltbox by the river, where her grandparents had lived all their lives. Just for a year, it was said, while Will finished his degree. No rent for them to pay, and he only needed to be in Cambridge twice a week. She can remember her dislike of the idea of living, however briefly, in that house, away from the city, in a place she'd spent months of her childhood, a house one branch or another of her family had lived in or owned for more than three centuries. The weight of the past felt so heavy there, it was hard to imagine a future. Will set his desk up in the parlor, next to the four-foot-high mahogany radio in whose bottom cabinets the old 78s of Beethoven and Mahler gathered their dust. Trying to read a book on the sofa in the afternoon, she had to work hard to forget the sight of her grandmother sitting in the chair opposite, napping through a summer rainstorm.

Before they were married they had talked about having children; they both wanted them. A bit of a strain, don't you think? her mother said when she brought up the idea, their life together having just begun, no job for Will yet. But Will didn't see any reason to wait. They were happy when she got pregnant. More than the wedding vows this meant permanence—a future they could predict.

"Beautiful morning," Mrs. Johnson says, poking her head in the door. She has been the director of Plymouth Brewster all the years Elizabeth has been here. A gentle redheaded woman who sits with Elizabeth and discusses the books she is reading. "Don't forget you've got a visitor this afternoon."

Elizabeth smiles and Mrs. Johnson passes on and Elizabeth gazes again over the harbor. She sees people, tiny at this distance, heading out along the breakwater, leaning into the wind as they go. Yachts bob in the marina, their chrome masts ticking back and forth like the arms of metronomes. Sun glistens on the water. The scene is alive with motion.

Nearly four hundred years since our family arrived on this shore, Hester begins, her voice cleaner and more vibrant this morning.

"Here we go," Elizabeth says, taking a seat in her chair, "sing your little song." It's better when she's able to affect nonchalance. Signs of care are like flesh exposed to her companion's arrows.

And what a beautiful season of suffering it has been. What principled wars. What tidy profit. And the machines, they are enough to take your breath away. And all the limbs and eyes and organs of the children bled and severed for progress. And the raped slaves and the heads of boy soldiers crushed like eggs. Why, the minister might even allow us a dance. Perhaps to celebrate you, Elizabeth, a flower grown from the seed of all this. What have you done to correct it? Do you suppose the divines would have liked your country club, Daddy coming down the back nine, dark hands fixing Mommy a cocktail? Jitterbug.

"Lousy historian," Elizabeth mutters, trying to maintain the dismissive upper hand. "You're confusing all sorts of things." It's been years since she's had to argue like this. She has the energy, for now.

I'd forgotten, Hester says. You always believed books and their facts could save you. Haven't done so well by them, have you?

Elizabeth laughs. "If I'd only known what a harsh woman you were."

What? You would have refused my help?

"Is that what you gave me?"

And then the memory is there, the morning her contractions began: second day of the blizzard, 1978, the roads covered in ice and buried, the police saying no one was to drive, the hospital telling them they weren't sure when they could send an ambulance. She lay upstairs in her grandparents' old room, in the front of the house.

For hours she did her breathing as best she could, laboring there on the high bed, clutching Will's hand. When the contractions got worse, her mother tended her, told her she had to be brave. Elizabeth begged for the doctor or drugs—something to blunt the vicious pain in her abdomen. In the moments of reprieve, she'd open her eyes and from the walls of the bedroom see the dead generations staring down at her: daguerreotypes of gaunt women and simian-faced men, stiff as iron in Sunday black, posed as if to meet their maker. As children visiting their grandparents, Elizabeth and her brother scared each other telling stories of the people who'd died in these rooms. The pictures seemed alive now, the ancestors' rectitude offended by her abjection. She bit her pillow and sweated. Hours passed and still no doctor. She heard Will and her parents whispering in the other room, saying, how could they move her now that she was so far along and the roads so dangerous?

At six the power went out, leaving the house in darkness. For a few minutes, all that remained of the world was the seizing pain and the rush of the wind lashing the trees in the front yard. Her father lit candles, put batteries in the radio. It kept snowing. From downstairs, she could hear the news saying hundreds of people were stranded in cars on the highway and then the voice of the announcer telling citizens to remain in their homes.

Her mother gave her water and wiped down her face and chest. The pictures flickered in the shadows. Past one in the morning, in the fifteenth hour, long after she'd started to push, her mother left for a moment to find more towels. Elizabeth lay on the soaked mattress alone, Will in the kitchen boiling water on the gas stove, her father yelling on the phone to the hospital, snow pressing against the glass, the flesh between her legs ripping. She felt blood leaking onto her thighs. Something started hammering at her temples. Her heart kicked. She thought she would die.

It was then she looked up in the candlelight and for the first time saw Hester standing in the far corner of that ancient, crooked, low-ceilinged room. She stood silent in her black dress and hooded cape, a woman of thirty with a face of fifty, plain featured, eyes of mild gray. Naive about nothing. A woman who had lain in this room on a winter night some centuries ago, Elizabeth understood, her husband at a trading post on the Connecticut River, her sister there to tend her, three younger children instructed not to cry, crying in the other room, twenty hours before she expired. A woman Elizabeth need give no explanation, her life reduced to a line in a letter written from one man to another. A line Elizabeth had always remembered from a summer past when her grandfather read them papers their ancestors had left in the house: *Sad past words to report Hester has died giving me a boy.*

Elizabeth stared at the dark figure in the corner and

would have cried out were it not for her worry that Will and her parents would think her crazy. Slowly and without a word, Hester walked to the bed. She placed a cold hand on Elizabeth's brow. Elizabeth closed her eyes. She sensed Hester's hands between her legs, holding the baby's head. She gave a final push. When she opened her eyes and strained upright, she saw the blue child. The umbilical cord had wrapped itself twice around his neck in her womb, pulling against his tiny throat, strangling him as he was born.

Will was the first to enter. In the instant before reason or compassion or duty retrieved him from the doubt of her sanity he must always have harbored, he stared at her as if at a murderer. In a rush, she explained how it happened, because what choice did she have then? How a woman had come and delivered the child, how the cord must have been coiled like that for weeks, and her parents wept and Will held his head in his hands. In the early morning, a nurse arrived and cut the boy loose.

"It's not help you gave me," Elizabeth says aloud from her chair by the window. "It's not help you gave."

She is thankful that for now there is no reply.

Thankful too that the colors in her room beat once again with the pulse of life, the air and the blue ocean quickening to a new birth. Sedation's cloud is lifted. And Ted, Ted will be here soon.

THAT AFTERNOON SHE hears his voice coming up the stairwell from the front desk. Judith, the nurse, has bought her the

Pepperidge Farm cookies she asked for and she's saved juice from lunch along with two glasses.

Soon, he knocks on the open door. "Hey there, Mrs. Maynard."

For years Mrs. Johnson has sent along the facility's information to the high school volunteer program, inviting students to sign up for regular visits with an appropriate resident. Every autumn one or two come, but Elizabeth has never been lucky enough to have someone assigned to her. Until now.

He's wearing a blue ski jacket she hasn't seen on him before. His curly brown hair hangs down over the jacket's high, puffy collar. The centers of his cheeks are red from the cold.

"You're beautiful," she says.

He glances back along the corridor, then down at the floor. "That's cool," he mutters.

"I got us come cookies. Would you like one?"

He steps into the room, shrugging off his knapsack. She holds the plate up and he takes three Milanos.

"Wow," he says, "you got a lot of my pictures up here. Did you have all these up last week?"

"I took down some of their dreadful watercolors so I have more room now. I like the portraits. They're very good."

"How was your week?" he asks.

Weirdly, the little brochure Ted got when he signed up for the volunteer program said this was the sort of question you weren't supposed to ask the residents, because usually their weeks did not vary and it was best to focus on positive things. Ted has decided this is a crock of shit and figures this woman has lived through a week as sure as anyone else.

"Oh, it was just *riveting,*" Elizabeth says with a big smile. "Gladys Stein nearly expired in the midst of a bridge tournament. She was upset with Dickie Minter telling stories about Mussolini."

He's learned it's okay to laugh at this stuff even if he doesn't get it.

"And the food?" he asks.

"Factory fresh."

They chuckle together, friends enjoying their joke.

"I kinda had this idea," Ted says. "I was thinking instead of me drawing today, we could go for a drive. Would you be into that?"

Since her parents died, Elizabeth's old friend Ginny is the only one who takes her out, down to Plymouth Harbor or for a walk on Duxbury Beach, no more than twice a year.

"That would be wonderful," she says.

Donning the fur coat and hat her grandmother gave her as a wedding present, she leads Ted down to Mrs. Johnson's office. There are only voluntary residents at Plymouth Brewster; it is no mental hospital with locked wards, but a place where people come to live structured lives. Elizabeth has never been much trouble to anyone at the facility. As long as they are back before dinner, Mrs. Johnson says, it would be fine.

"I USED TO drive a station wagon like this," she remarks as they pull onto a highway she has not seen before. "Has this road been here a long time?"

"I guess like, yeah, since before I was born."

Elizabeth laughs. "Ginny doesn't want to upset me, you see. They tell her familiarity is a good thing, so she takes me on the old roads. It would make sense if I were senile, I suppose, but really it is quite interesting to see this road."

Soon they will pave it all, every marsh and fen. The animals will die and we will die with them. How much must be destroyed before people are satisfied?

She is quite an environmentalist for a seventeenth-century woman, Elizabeth thinks, but a hypocrite too, she tries telling herself: remember the diseases you brought, dear, remember the dead natives.

You think you haven't profited from that? Hester stabs back.

"I was thinking maybe you could help me out with something," Ted says. Elizabeth looks across the seat at him. His hair is a mess. He hunches forward over the steering wheel, racked with a worry she finds adorable. She is here in the car with him. No slowing paste in the brain. Seconds come one after the other.

"By all means," she says. "What can I do?"

"Well see, there's this person—she's a girl. She goes to my school. And somebody told me it was her birthday soon . . ."

"You want to buy her something."

"Yeah," Ted says, relieved. "Yeah, exactly. But what?"

"I'm charmed that you would ask my advice," she says.

They pull off the first exit and into the parking lot of a giant mall, another place not ten miles from the Plymouth Brewster Elizabeth has never seen.

"We will find you the perfect gift," she says, stepping

from the car. "My mother was a great shopper. We would take the train down to New York and spend the afternoon picking out dresses at Bergdorf's and then we'd have tea at the Plaza and stay the night there and examine shoes in the morning." She barely recognizes the playful tone she hears in her voice. "I know a good piece of merchandise when I see it."

"Cool."

Elizabeth is able to dispense with the entirety of a store named T.J. Maxx in under five minutes. "Not us," she says, gliding into the sunlit atrium, amazed at how easy it is to be here among people.

"What's her name?"

"Lauren. But she's not exactly, at the moment, you know, like my girlfriend."

"Ah-hah, I see. Yes. This information is helpful. Here we are, good old Lord & Taylor, I think this will do nicely."

"Oh, yeah, and her family—they're rich. But what's cool is she didn't take a car from her parents, even though her stupid brother drives an SUV."

"And does she live in a grand house?"

"Yeah, it's pretty big. Down at the end of Winthrop Street, kinda near your old place. I've only driven by it a couple times."

They arrive at accessories, Elizabeth fighting nervous excitement, recalling suddenly that the Lesters gave her a leather wallet for her wedding, embossed with her new initials. The Lesters, who came all the way from San Francisco and sat in the third row at Saint Andrew's Church, and danced at the club after dinner: the men in black tie or officer's dress, the women in chiffon or silk, glittering beneath the chandeliers, champagne on the porch, the sloping landscape of the golf course visible in the summer evening light, all of it just a bit more than her father could afford but what he and everyone wanted.

"A wallet perhaps?" she asks. "Cordovan with a silver clasp?"

"It looks kinda like my mother's wallet. I mean, she's got a cool wallet and all, but—"

"Of course, you're right, we need something . . . contemporary."

"Do you think it's stupid to buy her something? I mean, she hasn't even gone out with me."

They pause briefly in luggage.

"What is it about her, Ted, what captivates you?"

"Well, she's only been at school since the beginning of the semester, so she has friends but not really a clique yet. And she's like an alterna-chick, you know, with her nose pierced, but real small, just a little stud, really tasteful, and her hair's short and she wears great clothes, I guess like Euro indy-pop clothes. But that's only part of it. I guess I just want to figure out what's in her head, you know. Something about her makes me want to figure that out."

Hester disapproves mightily of the cosmetics department. Strumpets hawking vanity: this is what we have become. A month of humiliation wouldn't cleanse the body spiritual.

"Days of humiliation went out a long time ago, deary," Elizabeth mutters, "and besides, they suffer too," she reminds her old companion, sensing the fatigue in the smiles of the brightly clad women behind the shimmering counters. And shimmer they do, so fiercely Elizabeth wishes she had brought her sunglasses: the way the light hits the polished steel and glass, the glare of the tall orange display of a football player and bride, the picture of an ocean coming at her from the left, the saleswoman's plucked eyebrow rising.

"Something for the holiday?"

Elizabeth breathes.

"Ted," she says, suddenly imploring the lights to dim, "why don't you explain to this nice lady."

His cheeks flush red. "Well, ah, actually Lauren doesn't wear makeup."

Hester has noticed a large sign on the counter announcing a Thanksgiving Day sale for something called Egoiste perfume. Above the picture of the man's naked torso there is a turkey in one corner and the cartoon of a pilgrim in the other.

"Don't be silly," Elizabeth says, "it's just a bit of kitsch."

"But I thought you said we'd get her something good," Ted says.

"Oh," Elizabeth replies, grabbing the nearest bar of lipstick, handing it to Ted. "How pretty that is, don't you think? I think it's pretty."

"Ma'am, what are you doing?" the saleswoman asks.

"Nothing, nothing, it's just that some people don't like this—" She has the sign now and is digging her fingers at the frame, trying to get at the poster, the sound of her fingernails extremely loud, the air all around beginning to hum.

"Lady—you can't do that."

"Stop shouting," she says.

"Mrs. Maynard," Ted says. "That's the store's display, maybe we should leave it there."

"I know, Ted, I'm sorry, I agree, it's just that it's a piece of trash and it offends people and it needs to be gotten rid of, even though we all know Thanksgiving is a nineteenth-century invention, so why she should object"—Elizabeth has it now and begins ripping—"I don't know, I guess the whole ego thing, just too much of it—"

"I'm calling security," the cosmetics lady announces in a voice octaves lower than a moment before.

"Come on," Ted says, taking Elizabeth's arm even as her hands tear the glossy paper into ever smaller pieces. He's afraid she'll start crying like she did the day a few weeks back when he showed her the picture he'd drawn of her. He gets them quickly out of the store and onto the escalator. She's finished ripping, no more poster left. She stares forward now in what appears to be dread. He's still got the lipstick in his hand but figures it doesn't have a detector strip so pockets it as they head for the exit to the parking lot.

Crossing to the car, Mrs. Maynard still resting her hand on his arm, he thinks of his mother, who sits alone upstairs all afternoon, all morning too, coming down only for dinner, barely saying a word, her face almost dead, and how his father and brother say nothing. None of them ever talk about her when they go to the movies on the weekends, or when the relatives come and she stays in her room, or when Ted has a play at school and all week she says tomorrow, I'll come tomorrow, and on Saturday night can't look him in the eye to say she won't make it. At first, Ted didn't want to come to Plymouth

Brewster as a volunteer. Enough already with the fucking mentally ill, for Christ's sake, enough, but something made him come, and then Mrs. Maynard, when she asked him to draw, and he got to sit there and draw and have her ask him questions about the books he was reading and what he wanted to do, and how his car sounded in the winter, and what oil he used, and how much he'd weighed when he was born, just to sit there and be asked a hundred stupid questions while he drew pictures: it was all somehow worth it.

"I'm sorry," Elizabeth calls out in a high-pitched voice as they get in the car.

"Don't worry," he insists, clenching the steering wheel. "Don't worry."

Mrs. Johnson sees them from her office as they enter the lobby. "Oh dear," she says. "What happened?"

"Nothing," Ted replies. "We went to a store, that's all. Mrs. Maynard, she decided she wanted to leave—nothing's the matter."

"Elizabeth?" the director asks. "Are you all right?"

She nods. "You must be tired," she says, turning to Ted. "You should go home and sleep."

"Sure," he says.

"Yes," Mrs. Johnson agrees, taking Elizabeth's arm, "it's time for your nap."

"DUUUDE," STEVIE PIPER calls out that night, "check *this* out." The bottom of a plastic gallon milk container has been cut off with a bread knife, a foil screen placed over its mouth,

the Davidsons' kitchen sink filled to the brim, the bottomless container lowered into the water, the pot lit on the screen, Stevie now slowly raising the handle, the motion drawing smoke down into the milk jug, which comes to hold an immense, dense cloud of marijuana. Stevie removes the foil, Ted puts his lips over the jug's mouth, following it suddenly downward as Stevie plunges the handle into the water, the air pressure forcing the huge mass of smoke straight into Ted's lungs, sending him reeling backward from the sink, against the corner of the granite countertop, into Heather Trackler, his feet catching on a half-full double bowl of cat food and milk, sending him onto the black-and-white tile, smoke billowing from his mouth, his butt hitting the strip heater with a harsh metallic crunch.

"Domestic FUCKING bliss!" Stevie cries, throwing his arms in the air as though he's just crossed the finishing line of some Olympic event conducted entirely in his own head. He begins rejigging the hydraulic mechanism for another round.

"Oh my *God,* you guys," Heather says, wiping Sprite off her cashmere sweater. "People live here."

"You know what?" Stevie says. "I bet they fucking do."

Ted nods apologetically, his mind beginning to sail.

Lauren walks into the kitchen. He looks up at her from the floor, his hand splayed in a pool of milk, cat food all around him. He raises his hand to wave, feeling liquid drip down his arm.

"Looks like you're having fun," she says.

He experiences an overwhelming sense of gratitude that she is still wearing the orange cardigan.

"*Duude.* You gotta get up outta that food over there, man, don't let it waylay you, don't get detained by it."

With Stevie's encouragement, Ted rises and suddenly he and Lauren are face-to-face, as if conversation were now supposed to ensue.

Stevie gazes at the two of them and with the wily eye of a stoner clocks their little tension. "So do you—," he begins, but unable to manage, dissolves into a fit of laughter. They watch him because he is something to watch that is not each other. "So do you come here often?" he finally gets out, folding over in hysterics, slapping the counter, weeping.

"You're *such* a loser," Heather says. "Come on, you guys, let's go upstairs," and she leads them up the back staircase onto a landing, from where, through another open door, they can see a fully clothed boy standing in a nearly overflowing bathtub swatting at a floating house plant with a tennis racket, cheered on in his novel sport by three other boys gesticulating furiously, tubside.

"This is all so meaningless and destructive," Heather says.

Ted risks a sideways glance at Lauren and is rendered momentarily inoperative by the realization that she was in fact already looking at him when he glanced, this causing their eyes to meet. At lunch—what seems a thousand years ago—she grinned twice at comments he made and none of her friends laughed.

Heather announces she is going to put an end to the bathroom vandalism and marches across the landing, calling out ahead of her, "Hey there!" leaving Ted and Lauren alone by the banister. Acid house pumps from the living room up into the brightly lit stairwell.

Stevie has advised Ted that if he finds himself toasted and needs to simulate normal conversation, he should adopt a simple compare-and-contrast strategy: state an uncontroversial fact about yourself—who you have for history, what you did last summer, et cetera—followed by a question eliciting the same information from the other person. This is what people do in real life, Stevie always says. Just behave as if the given circumstances were real. The method seems partially effective until the music changes abruptly to Lou Reed, at which point Ted becomes convinced all remaining facts about his life *are* deeply controversial.

"Sorry Stevie was such an asshole," he says.

"Whatever. You're not joined at the hip."

Lauren's casual eloquence stuns him. "You're right," he says, "we're not."

Caged longing presses up through his chest and into his throat. He wants to tell her he's never had a girlfriend, never even had sex, only been kissed twice, and that this makes him feel like an ugly creature and a freak, but he concludes these thoughts are better kept to himself.

"I love your sweater," he says.

"Thanks."

"And I like that thing on your neck—what is it?"

"Jade," she says, touching it with her fingers.

"I bet it's warm. It must get warm when it hangs on your neck."

"This is criminal!" Heather yells from the bathroom. "You'll do time for this."

"You want to sit down?" Lauren asks.

"Okay," he says.

They cross the landing into what looks to be a guest room. Lauren flops down onto a large white sofa. "I bet the Davidsons are drinking piña coladas in some beach hut on Aruba."

"Yeah," Ted agrees, "talking to friends about their good son Jack applying early admission."

"Exactly."

"My parents never go away," he says. "Do yours?"

"Sometimes. They're trite. They care about silly things."

"Harsh."

"Yeah," she says. "It is."

Ted perches on the edge of the couch. "You seem older."

She turns to look at him, her eyes slightly narrowed, slightly blurred.

"What do you mean?"

"It's like you've experienced all this before. The way you don't talk much, but like you're thinking something instead, something you're not saying. It's odd." He would like to put his hand behind her head and let it rest in his palm, perhaps taste the jade lozenge hanging round her neck. He wonders what he would know about her if they touched.

"I'm stoned," he says, leaning back into the sofa. "If I say weird stuff, you won't be offended, will you?"

She shakes her head. "I'm drunk."

Ted closes his eyes. He sees Mrs. Maynard asleep in her

room up on the hill. He's never mentioned to his parents or his brother that he visits her, but then they've never asked about the program he signed up for.

"I went to this store today," he says, "with this woman I visit over in Plymouth, for the volunteer thing. I draw for her usually, but we went out today. She kind of flipped out in the store. She ripped up this poster they had, and then . . ." He sees Mrs. Maynard's face as she gazed, terrified, onto the highway ahead of them. "In the car she told me there was a woman sitting in the backseat, but that I shouldn't look because she was angry. She said she heard the woman's voice a lot but she only saw her once in a while."

He opens his eyes and looks at Lauren. "The strange thing is," he says, "I wasn't scared. I mean, it was creepy, but I believed her."

"You thought there was really another person in your car that you couldn't see?"

"For her there was, yeah."

To this Lauren makes no reply. They sit on the couch a while, listening to Lou Reed singing from downstairs. The borderline defeat in his voice seems alien to the objects in the room: the coffee table books, the dried flowers, the waffle-patterned bed skirts, the beige clock and ruffled curtains—these things they're supposed to want one day. The objects persist blandly in the bland intention of their owners. For Ted, they have the sadness of the things in his own house, the maple living room set his parents bought the year he was born, the dining room table they used to sit at when he was younger, reminders of old marital hope. He and Lauren are just florid detritus in a room like this, drifting past on the dead river of time that never ceases here.

"I like you," Lauren says.

Suddenly, Ted's heart crashes into his rib cage. He hears George Clooney yell, "Lidocaine!" sees himself sped on a gurney toward a team of doctors, bright lights, IV drips, and he knows he is very high and all of a sudden absolutely happy.

"That's *so* cool," he says to her. "I got you some lipstick."

And then Heather is standing in front of them, rage of a prosecutor emblazoned on her face, and she says she's leaving, there's another party at the Putnams', and if they want a ride they better come.

11

THE HOLIDAYS BRING Christmas lights and family visits to Plymouth Brewster, along with the news that Mrs. Johnson is retiring at the end of the year. The new man, Mr. Attwater, young and handsome in a boring sort of way, wears dark suits and shakes everyone's hand. The older women coo, the younger women are suspicious, the men play cards. Rehearsals for *Our Town* keep Ted from coming the first two weeks of December, though he calls to tell Elizabeth and says he's sorry.

The second time he phones they speak a long while. Ted sounds reluctant to hang up. Finally, Elizabeth steels her courage and asks, "Have you seen Lauren?" They have not mentioned their trip to the mall.

"Yeah," he replies with the quick, breathless voice she's come to recognize as his unconscious signal of interest. "Yeah, she's in the play. I get to narrate what she does and stuff."

"I'm sorry, Ted, that we didn't get her a gift."

"Oh no, that's cool. I actually gave her the lipstick anyway. She was kinda into it." He pauses. "I've been sort of wondering, like when you were married . . ."

"Yes?"

"Or like before that, when you guys were dating . . . I mean at some point, you guys, like, got together so you must have let him know when it was cool to do that, right?"

"That's right," Elizabeth says. "He would call the dorm. I would tell him if I were free on the evening he suggested. He was very reliable in that regard. He always called when he said he would. You should remember that, Ted. Politeness is a tremendous asset."

"Yeah, right," he says. "But like after that, I mean after you decided to hang out, did you let him know when other stuff should happen, or did he kinda . . . let you know?"

"Oh. I see. You mean about sex."

She can almost feel his wince at the other end of the line; she restrains a giggle.

"Yes," he whispers.

"I'm afraid I'm not much of one to ask about these things. But you're a good person. You're kind. Be kind to her."

"Okay."

The next time he calls he tells her it's coming up for winter break at the high school, and with performances and things he and the other volunteer won't be back until January. Elizabeth hadn't been told about a break over the vacation, and she takes it hard. But Ted calls each week, once on Christmas, and with this she thinks she will get by until the day he returns.

Judith, the nurse, has grown suspicious of her behavior over the last few weeks, hearing her talk sometimes, and Elizabeth has begun flushing her Primidone down the toilet rather than risk discovery. She's been on the drugs so long she's forgotten many ordinary satisfactions. What cold water feels like in a parched mouth. The pleasure concentration on a single thought can yield. The days bring with them the pulse, the hum, joyous sometimes, terrifying others, but alive, full and alive. And they bring Hester, never now a day without her.

In the midst of it all, there is so much she wants to ask Ted that she's started making a list so she won't forget.

NEW YEAR'S EVE begins with a clear, bright sky, flooding Elizabeth's room in light. The annual party is scheduled for after dinner. Families will drop by in the early evening and everyone will be in bed by ten. It is Mrs. Johnson's last day as director and she makes the rounds of the rooms saying goodbye. Some of these men and women she's known twenty-five years. It's just after lunch, as the sky clouds over and snow begins to fall, that she comes to Elizabeth. They start as they always do by Mrs. Johnson reporting what she's been reading—a book written by a foreigner about traveling in America, she says, full of suggestions for places to visit. She and her husband plan a trip across the country in the spring. She's never been to the South and wants to go.

To snap pictures of plantations and muse at the faded grandeur of it all, I suppose. What a blissful forgetting it must be.

In the mornings, it is easier to reply without speaking aloud (at night it has become impossible), so Elizabeth tells Hester to be quiet, which for the moment she is.

There is a sad expression on Mrs. Johnson's face and Elizabeth wonders if she actually wants to retire, or if perhaps she has been made to by others.

"You haven't been in touch with your husband, have you?" she says. It is odd that Mrs. Johnson should ask this question. Elizabeth hasn't spoken to Will in more than twenty years. He lives in California with a wife and three children. Mrs. Johnson knows this well enough.

"No," Elizabeth says.

"And Ginny, she's never mentioned anything about other arrangements?"

"Is something the matter? Do I have to leave?"

Mrs. Johnson shakes her head. "It's just that the new director and I have been reviewing things. I'm sure he's right, there are issues of liability, legal things we have to be careful about. There was concern about your outing with Ted.

"Elizabeth, I tried to convince him otherwise, but Mr. Attwater's decided that as long as you're here, you're not to have visits from a volunteer. God knows it's the last thing I wanted to tell you today, but I wanted it at least to be me who told you."

Elizabeth tilts her head to one side. "No visits?"

Mrs. Johnson folds her hands in her lap.

"I see," Elizabeth says. "Mr. Attwater. He's decided."

"Yes."

HE CANNOT EVEN commence an attempt to concentrate on the Arnold Schwarzenegger movie. As he sits in the cinema with Lauren on one side and Heather and Stevie, who've started dating, on the other, the deep irrelevance of the movie strikes him like an epiphany. In a few hours he, Ted, will be naked in a bed with a girl he loves, and the whole miserable material world seems a mighty petty thing in comparison to this. It seems it might never matter again. The date has been set for a week, her Christmas present to him whispered in his ear, the whole thing so damn sophisticated he feels like one of those men in top hat and tails who dance on moonlit balconies in the black-and-white movies his parents used to watch. "Suave" is the word.

Finally, the stupid flick ends and they follow the crowd out into the parking lot, where the snow has begun to fall heavily now and the plows have started their work for the night.

"You guys coming to the party?" Heather asks.

Ted squints, shrugs, looks off into the distance. "Sounds kinda cool, I'm thinking maybe not, though, you know. It's getting late."

"Hello? It's New Year's Eve."

Lauren, dressed in sheer black club pants and a simple

black leather jacket, interrupts Ted's nonchalance by informing the others that her parents are away and she and Ted are going back to her place—no interruption of his hipness, he realizes, but a cubing of it.

"What do you think, Heather?" Stevie asks, rolling onto the balls of his feet. "Maybe you and me could go play some cops and robbers too."

Heather gives a mocking snort. "Please. I'll probably be bailing you out when you get arrested with your gay little drugs."

"Have fun," Lauren says, taking Ted's hand, something she's never done in front of other people. Instantly, he has an erection. As they walk toward his car, he wonders how premature premature ejaculation is, if men come miles from their girlfriends' homes, if they'll make it to her house in time.

On the highway, Lauren puts in an ambient house tape, a slow beat, the volume way down. Wet flakes zoom into the windshield out of the dark hills of the sky. The mall lots they pass are lit and empty. The stores are closed, the car dealerships vanishing beneath the snow. Tonight, Ted doesn't see this familiar landscape as a present fact, but already as a memory, a scene he will one day recall. It's strange and exciting to perceive things from such a distance. He glimpses how beautiful even this world can be if you aren't actually in it.

On the passenger's side, Lauren sits quietly, her leather jacket unzipped, the orange cardigan they've joked about buttoned underneath it. Her face has an oddly purposeful expression, her eyes fixed on the dashboard. In the month they've been going out, there's been a fair amount of silence between them, which Lauren doesn't seem to mind, though it makes Ted anxious. They've talked about her family some. At first he thought she loathed her parents in the way some of his other wealthy friends do, with a kind of casual cynicism, as if their mothers and fathers were minor officials in the national corruption—illegitimate people living illegitimate lives. He's always thought with bitterness it was a luxury to view your parents this way—as people strong enough to withstand your derision. But the more time he spends with Lauren, the more he thinks she understands this, that she could hurt her parents. Her determination, her careful plan for their getting together, it's about something different, about being in control.

Her house is a six-month-old mock château with a three-car garage, a fountain, and a turret. Inside, it's wired like a spaceship: thermostats, alarms, humidifiers, key pads to control it all. Most of the time half the shit is broken, the living room tropical, the doorbell not even working. Her father spends evenings yelling at contractors. His work has something to do with money. They're down at their condo in Florida this weekend with Lauren's brother.

"Want a glass of wine?" she asks when they get into the kitchen.

"Yeah," he says, "that would be cool."

The high-ceilinged room is an odd combination of expensive chrome appliances and peeling wood furniture that looks like it was bought at a yard sale.

As Lauren hands Ted his glass, she leans forward to kiss

him gently on the lips, a touch he receives, as always, weak kneed and nervous. He puts his free arm around her. He tries not to think about this evening in his own house, his brother out with friends, his father reading the paper in the living room, alone, his mother upstairs in bed, alone, their empty kitchen smelling slightly of the cleaning spray his father will have used on the counters after making dinner and washing the dishes.

"What's up with the table?" he says.

"Having decrepit old shit you pay through the nose for is the latest thing. They can't get enough of it. Perverse, isn't it?"

Ted supposes that it is. She leans her head into the hollow of his shoulder and puts her hand in his back pocket, palming the cheek of his ass. He thinks they better hurry. Be kind to her, Mrs. Maynard said. He imagines he's the only kid at his school who gets his romantic advice from a schizophrenic.

Taking his hand, Lauren leads him through rooms of fine rugs and distressed furniture, chandeliers and gilt-framed paintings, up a staircase wide enough to sleep on.

TIRES OF PASSING cars send arcs of snow into the air, dotting the skirt of her coat. She pauses now and then to wipe the fur clean with her gloved hands. Several inches have already accumulated on the road's shoulder, but she manages all right in her boots, huffing a bit as she goes, unused to the exertion of a walk longer than the circumference of the grounds. In the hubbub of the New Year's party, no one noticed her leaving.

Headlights flash up into her eyes, pass, and vanish. Wind

drives snow down out of the sky. She reaches an intersection and sees it's the old Plymouth Road, gas stations on three corners now. She turns north, ears full of the storm and Hester's voice.

You should have heard the animals dying that winter in the cold, how the horse groaned in the frost, sheep starving in their pens, snow past the windows. And you know my eldest died of her cough in my arms when the ground was covered and too hard to bury her, so she lay under a sheet in the woodshed, where for a month I saw her every time I went to gather fuel for our fire. And we weren't the worst off, sick at least with diseases we knew.

"I don't care," Elizabeth says, though it isn't true and she can't help seeing Hester in the woodshed. Her responses go unheeded now in any case. She starts up a rise she can remember being driven along by her grandfather in his Packard.

Eighty years the owners of a sawmill and merchants through the Revolution, and of course, you know the cellar was fitted with a second cellar covered with a boulder lowered from an oak beam by rope, where our family hid during raids by the British, relying on the appointed neighbor—should he survive—to come and lift the stone when the soldiers had quit their burning. And merchants still in the early days of the Republic, selectmen at town hall, teachers, a judge, a colonel, a daughter ended in the river, never mentioned, a graveyard full of us.

On the sidewalk, she shakes her head back and forth, back and forth. "I know this. What does it matter?"

Witnesses by news and action to the slaughters here and abroad; money in the banks that made the wars; snobbery; polite unspoken belief in the city on the hill and our place at its center; disdain; a preference for distant justice; lives of comfort made from other people's labor; and don't tell me it doesn't matter, that it's all too complex now, because it isn't and you know it and we always have. One eye on heaven, the other blind.

At the top of the rise, Elizabeth sees the factory where they make cranberry juice and she remembers walking in the fields behind the house with Will, past the old bogs, thinking to herself how they would one day walk those paths with their child, how once he was born, life would be about the future. The oval Ocean Spray insignia is painted in red and blue on the side of the building, perched there on the shore against the icy, churning sea.

Farther from the center of town, traffic lights hang over deserted intersections. She walks on and on past fields and houses, another group of stores, a liquor market, a fast food restaurant. She crosses the town line out of Plymouth and keeps going, the snow coming faster. At the highway overpass there is no more Howard Johnson's, some other motel now.

"He's out this evening," Ted's father said when she called from her room. Then she remembered him telling her he and Lauren were spending New Year's together. At the end of Winthrop Street, he'd said her place was, the day they visited Lord & Taylor.

Brickman's Funeral Home is still there, and the Catholic

church, and the convenience store at the top of the hill. Crossing the river, she walks by the old shoe factory, shops and apartments now, built on the ground of the ancient sawmill. She can barely feel her cheeks in the cold as she turns down her family's street.

The old house sits back from the road, steep front roof with the long sloping back covered in a layer of white; weathered shingles detached in places; the shutters the same dark red they've always been. Her brother has never been able to bring himself to sell it, so it's rented to people who usually don't stay long. The crab apple tree still stands in the front yard, buffeted by the winds of another snow, and she thinks the house looks much as it must have the night she lay upstairs in the front room.

Once the doctor told Will and her parents that a third of babies were born with the cord wrapped once around the neck—twice less often but not never—whatever unspoken suspicion they had ended. But the trouble was Hester didn't leave that night. She stayed. And occasionally Elizabeth couldn't help yelling at her for not uncoiling her son as a midwife would. After a week, Will left to see his family. Her parents took her to the psychiatrist.

In the fields she used to play in as a child—sold now—there are other homes, outsized in every way, their wide circular drives paved, lights sprayed down over the yards as if from the walls of prisons. Huge, gaudy places that dwarf the crumbling saltbox.

At the end of the street, she sees Ted's car parked in front of the blue imitation of a château. She walks up the drive, past an empty fountain.

"WHAT ABOUT YOUR room?" he asks, passing it in the hall.

She shakes her head. "We'll use my parents'."

They enter a room with dark satin walls, a canopy bed, undistressed, the carpet thick and plush. Lauren goes straight over and pulls the comforter off, throwing it onto the floor, leaving just the white sheets and lots of pillows. He wishes they were at least a bit drunk. This premeditation is unnerving.

Standing beside the bed, they start to kiss. It's harder than they've kissed before, their teeth knock, their tongues squirrel deep into each other's mouths. The remove Ted felt on the highway is with him here again, his mind somewhere behind them, committing the scene to memory. She takes his hand, puts it on her breast. He starts unbuttoning her shirt, wondering if he's moving too fast, but her hands are rubbing the small of his back in encouragement and he guesses this is how it is done. The material is silky to the touch and the buttons come apart easily. When he has her shirt off, Lauren reaches over her shoulders and removes her bra. Her breasts are small, her nipples darker than he expected. He's not sure what to do. Neither of them is moving. He has no erection and doesn't know why. She bites her lip and stares at the floor.

"Don't you want to do this?" she asks.

Suddenly, awfully, she doesn't seem older. Her knowing expression is gone. Replaced by awkwardness or confusion, maybe even anger, he can't tell. He feels alone. There's a half-naked stranger in front of him. He's the desperate guy he always imagined he was. Being here feels wrong, but somehow too late. He's supposed to know how things go and he doesn't. He leans down and tries kissing the side of her face, which works more or less, their bodies moving closer, her breasts warm through his shirt. He never imagined she might not have done this before. The thought terrifies him.

"Yeah," he replies, "of course."

He sits on the edge of the bed and Lauren starts undoing his shirt. He doesn't want to take his T-shirt off, but she tugs at the back of it, so he pulls it over his head, exposing his slender chest. They shift farther onto the mattress and he lies back. He's expecting her to climb up and kiss him but she doesn't. She unzips his jeans, which finally gives him his hard-on back. It's almost as he imagined it: her on top of him, this inscrutable look on her face, only it's not distance, nothing like that, and he's not asking her about where she's been or what it's like to come back from faraway places, even though these childish questions are the ones he still wants to ask. He thought somehow he would ask them now. But neither of them speak. There is the weight of her crushing his leg, a mole his fingers discover on the back of her shoulder as she kisses his stomach. It is weakness and helplessness he feels as she pulls down his jeans and boxers. They haven't talked about sex, only Christmas night outside her house, as her parents watched from the kitchen and she waved to them and then turned to Ted and whispered, *New Year's, let's do it then.* Naked now before her, he wants to ask if he is actually male in the way other men are, or if he is missing something he's never been able to see. His back arches sharply at the moist warm touch of her mouth on the head of his penis and he senses he can't let her do this or it will be over, so he pulls her up by her armpits and rolls her onto her back. He looks at her mouth but avoids her eyes. Still they say nothing. Lauren slips off her pants and underwear. She makes no sound as he leans down to kiss her nipples, but once he's started, she puts her hands in his hair and guides his head into her chest. He shudders at the taste of salt on her flesh. For an instant, he's poised between drive and revulsion. He licks her breast. She presses his face harder against her skin. He *wants* it now, his whole body *wants* it. With his elbows, he presses against the inside of her knees, spreading her legs.

"Put it on," she whispers. He leans back to grab from his jeans the condom he bought that morning. He's never used one before but he's seen pictures; he rolls it on as fast as he can. Then he crawls forward and she takes his penis in her hand. There are long, hideously awkward seconds as she squiggles farther down on the bed and he tries to push. His eyes are clenched shut. He hopes hers are too. Lauren takes a sudden, sharp breath, shouts, "Ow!" He holds himself above her.

"It's okay," he says. "I can stop."

"No," she says, her voice so deep and determined he

doesn't recognize it. She puts her hand on his butt and pulls. He can feel her trembling. Her breath is short and tight as he uses the muscles in the backs of his legs to move in and then almost out of her. It feels involuntary. Beastlike. Good. He begins to shiver and then with no warning comes in a rush, collapsing down onto her, burying his sighs in the pillow over her shoulder.

For a few seconds he lies across her, then rises, slipping out of her, leaning back onto his ankles. She covers herself with a pillow. He feels a wave of misery and defeat.

"Are you okay?" he whispers.

Her expression is blank, a little stunned. As though she has arrived somewhere only to discover it is no different than the place she has come from.

He leans to kiss her, but she turns her head. A bit of the lipstick he gave her is smeared across her cheek. He wonders why she ever decided to wear it. They remain there on the bed, neither of them moving. Hot air streams from a vent somewhere on the floor. His lips are dry and cracked.

From beneath the pillow, he notices a dark red stain seeping along the sheet. Looking down he sees his crotch is dark and wet. Lauren moves quickly off the mattress, wrapping herself in a towel, hurriedly moving to the bathroom. She closes the door behind her. He's kneeling there, on this enormous bed, staring into a circle of blood.

THREE TIMES SHE presses the bell, but there is neither sound nor answer. The downstairs lights are on, the shades up, snow visible as it drops through the squares of brightness into the bushes. She is cold and would like to be inside. Trying the latch, she finds it unlocked.

"Hello?" she calls, standing in the huge front hall, beneath a sparkling chandelier. "Ted?" The only reply is a click followed by the soft rumble of the furnace.

The walk has tired her. She passes into the dining room looking for a place to rest. The table needs painting, though it looks like a fine, sturdy old piece of furniture. She sits at the near end, taking off her hat, opening her coat. They have gone for a walk, she decides, young lovers in the snow, walking this ground she used to play on. She feels herself kneeling on the veranda, her arms around Peck, the shaggy mutt, holding him as he barks at a bird in the yard, feeling the bark's reverberations in her chest, her brother yelling at a friend up in the copper beech, the drone of the mower in the back field, air scented with grass; and she wrestles on the lawn with her father, trying to pry a coin from his fist. Her fingers run over the dent in his thumbnail; her mother says, *Watch it, you two,* leaning down to kiss her father. On the floor of the upstairs landing is a grate just above where her grandmother sits at her desk, and with her ear against it, crouched on the floorboards, Elizabeth hears the steel nib of her grandmother's ink pen scratching the thick card stock she writes her thank-you notes on. She is playing by herself upstairs. The bedspreads have patterns of tufted cotton. The posts of her grandparents' bed are of dark red cherry wood, tops carved in the shape of pineapples. Standing on the corner of the mattress, grasping the bedpost, her heels sink lower than the balls of her feet, stretching the joints of her ankles. The knife she uses to stab at the wood is the knife her grandfather uses to carve roast chicken on Sundays. Beneath the quick jabs of the silver tip spots of lighter red blossom in the dark varnish. Her heart beats so fast she can hardly breathe. Her mother shuts her in the guest room and in the evening her father spanks her over the edge of the couch, though she tells him she didn't want to do it. The marks are still on the posts of the bed there in the candlelight, as the snow falls, and she lies grasping her mother's hand, wishing the doctor would come to make her baby safe.

She wonders what other people's lives are like.

Ted halts at the entrance to the dining room, slack jawed. Mrs. Maynard sits in her fur coat at the far end of the table, staring out the window, a bleary, ruined look on her face.

"Mrs. Maynard?"

Elizabeth turns to see Ted standing in the door to the living room. He's not wearing a shirt, only jeans. His hair is as messy as she's ever seen it.

"Mrs. Maynard, what are you doing here? How did you get here? What's going on?"

"I thought you'd gone for a walk," she says. "It's snowing, you know. I thought you and Lauren were on a walk." She looks about the room as if searching for something. "I used to play on the ground this house is built on. Did you know that? Some say this place is an offense—ugly—that most all of what we've done since the beginning is ugly. But you're not, Ted. I told you. You're beautiful. The dead don't remember you. It's better that way. Will you come here and sit?"

Ted watches Mrs. Maynard lean forward and pull a dining room chair up beside her. She's had some kind of break, he thinks. The woman must be with her. He crosses to the chair and sits.

From her coat pocket, Elizabeth takes the folded piece of notepaper on which she's kept her list of questions. She pauses, then reading from the page, asks in a quiet voice, "Did you ever think you meant more to your mother than her own life?"

It's some nonsense she's written down, Ted says to himself. He still can't figure out how she got here. He'll have to drive her back.

"I'll just read them, Ted, and then you can . . . What is your mother's name?"

The roads will be bad by now; he doesn't have snow tires. It will take time.

"Mrs. Maynard—"

"Do you exist as a judgment of her? What does it feel like to be in her arms?"

Ted would like her to be quiet now. There is so much to think about. For ten minutes he stood by the bathroom door, calling softly, "Are you all right?" but Lauren said nothing, and all he could think of was her disappointment.

"Can you see your mother's face, or is it so familiar you don't see it? Do you feel that you know her?"

Elizabeth looks up and sees tears running from Ted's impassive eyes. She puts aside her list and lifts her hands to his cheeks. At her touch, his mouth trembles and he starts to sob.

You and all the inheritors of wealth who think life is a matter of perfected sentiment. You are wrong.

Elizabeth is exhausted. She does not argue. The lights in the room stream into her eyes like refulgent dawn. At last, she feels the warmth of her son's tears in the palms of her hands.

ACKNOWLEDGMENTS

FOR THEIR SUPPORT during the writing of this book, I would like to thank the Provincetown Fine Arts Work Center, the Michener/Copernicus Society of America, and the MacDowell Colony. I would also like to thank my editor Nan Talese, my agent Ira Silverberg, Frank Conroy, Marilynne Robinson, and Connie Brothers at the Iowa Writers' Workshop, Sandy McClatchy at *The Yale Review,* and Adrienne Brodeur and

Samantha Schnee at *Zoetrope* for their encouragement. For helping to improve various stories in this book, I owe thanks to Allan Gurganus, Nick Sywak, Minna Proctor, Justin Tussing, and Jacob Molyneaux. Finally, for making sure I left the apartment now and again, my thanks to Adam Hickey and David Grewal.

A NOTE ABOUT THE AUTHOR

ADAM HASLETT is a graduate of Swarthmore College and the Iowa Writers' Workshop. His work has appeared in *Zoetrope All-Story, The Yale Review, BOMB* magazine, and National Public Radio's *Selected Shorts* series. He has been a finalist for a National Magazine Award and has received fellowships from the Provincetown Fine Arts Work Center and the Michener/Copernicus Society of America. He is currently a student at Yale Law School.

A NOTE ABOUT THE TYPE

This book is typeset in Simoncini Garamond.
This version of Garamond was designed by
Francesco Simoncini and W. Bliz between 1958 and 1961,
for the Italian type foundry Simoncini.
Variations of Garamond have been a standard among
book designers and printers for four centuries; nearly every
manufacturer of type or typesetting equipment has produced at least
one version of Garamond in the past eighty years. The name is
attributed to sixteenth-century printer, publisher, and type designer
Claude Garamond, whose types were modeled on
those of Venetian printers from the end of the previous century.